ZACH KING

MY MAGICAL LIFE

Illustrated by
BEVERLY ARCE

KING

MY MAGICAL LIFE

PUFFIN

PUFFIN BOOKS

UK | USA | Canada | Ireland | Australia
India | New Zealand | South Africa

Puffin Books is part of the Penguin Random House group of companies
whose addresses can be found at global.penguinrandomhouse.com.

www.penguin.co.uk
www.puffin.co.uk
www.ladybird.co.uk

First published in the United States of America by HarperCollins
Children's Books and in Great Britain by Puffin Books 2017

001

Copyright © Zach King, 2017

Jacket art and interior illustrations by Beverly Arce

The moral right of the author and illustrator has been asserted

Set in 11.64/20.88 pt Sabon by Jouve (UK), Milton Keynes
Typography by Joe Merkel
Printed in Italy by LEGO SpA

A CIP catalogue record for this book is available from the British Library

ISBN: 978–0–141–38757–4

All correspondence to:
Puffin Books
Penguin Random House Children's
80 Strand, London WC2R 0RL

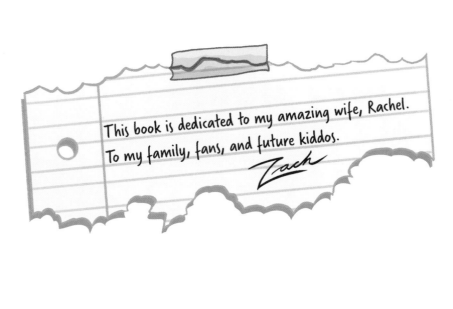

This book is dedicated to my amazing wife, Rachel.
To my family, fans, and future kiddos.

Zach

ZACH'S
KING-DOM

Michael the cat
- Perfect in every way
- Afraid of heights
so cute
Michael
AMAZING!
Marvelous!
WONDERFUL!
fantastic!
look! he signed
OMG. look @ his lil

gross
Tricia Stands
- Mean
- Popular?! (how?)
- likes attention
yeah
TRICIA
Where do you find all these stickers?
Internet
- Is 11 years old

The Kings (zach's fam)
one to rule them all!
Mom has a magic ring
Dad has a magic watch
funny
sma
DAD
Sophie
MOM
Sophie is Zach's little sister
Sophie has magic glasses

THE ADVENTURE BEGINS. . . .

CHAPTER 1

"Just one more try, please?"

Zach King sat on a swivel chair, hunched over a counter full of seemingly ordinary household objects—a light-up yo-yo, an old umbrella, a twenty-four-foot tape measure, a pair of fuzzy dice, and a snow globe from San Francisco. One of these, Zach felt sure, had to be his magical object. He pushed his black hair out of his eyes and looked up at his teacher, who also happened to be his dad. They were in the basement of his home. The Kings lived at the end of a private road, down a long, overgrown gravel driveway, in an ordinary-looking white and red farmhouse. Their home wasn't hidden, per se, but you definitely had to know where to look if you wanted to find it.

Zach's parents had converted the downstairs into a classroom for Zach and his younger sister, Sophie. They were both homeschooled, because their family wasn't like most other families—and Zach and Sophie weren't supposed to grow up to be like other kids. The Kings were magic. Their entire family—from both of Zach's parents to his aunts, uncles, cousins, and nephews. Everyone was magical, it seemed, except for Zach. He was already eleven, and try as he might, day after day after day, he had yet to find his magical thing, the object that would unlock his magic abilities.

Zach looked out the sliding-glass window, which offered a view of their backyard. He saw his mother setting up picnic tables for tomorrow's big family reunion. Zach was absolutely determined to figure out what his magic was before his whole extended family arrived.

"I don't know." Mr. King glanced at his old-fashioned wristwatch, a bronze timepiece with a faded engraving of an eagle in the center. It was his father's magic object.

He could use that wristwatch to turn back time. "Maybe we should call it a day. I promised your mother that I'd help her get ready for the party tomorrow."

"C'mon, Dad," Zach pleaded. "One more try, that's all I'm asking for."

"All right," Mr. King said, giving in. "I suppose I can make time for one more go."

Mr. King furrowed his brows and slowly gave his watch dial a turn. Zach felt that familiar static-like tingle as he noticed the clouds outside reverse course and roll back past the sun. The glass of juice that Zach had just drunk filled back up. The apple he'd snacked on became magically whole again. The digital display on the entertainment center started counting backward, while the hands on an antique cuckoo clock turned *counter*clockwise. A carved wooden cuckoo bird flapped backward above Zach's head before returning to its house-shaped clock. And like that, Zach and his Dad had a few extra minutes to find Zach's magic.

He focused his attention on a shiny silver flashlight and lifted it out of the box like he was picking up a sharpened sword.

"This is it," he said hopefully. "I know it!"

"Maybe," Mr. King said. "Give it a shot."

Zach took a deep breath and switched on the flashlight. He swept the beam over everything in sight, waiting for something *amazing* to happen. He had no idea what exactly he was hoping the flashlight could do, but it *had* to have some sort of magical power. It had to!

Zach gripped it tightly in both hands. He focused all his energy out of himself and into it, just like his parents had taught him to do. He imagined the flashlight cutting through solid objects like a laser blade and then having X-ray powers. He wanted it so badly to work, but it didn't. The flashlight was just a flashlight. It just lit things up.

"Oh well," Mr. King. "It was worth a try."

"No, wait!" Zach gripped the flashlight even tighter; his hands were starting to hurt. "Give it time. . . ."

The flashlight's beam landed on a vacuum cleaner resting in a corner. All at once, the vacuum roared to life. The vacuum started zooming around the room by itself, its headlights glowing like cat's eyes. Zach dropped the flashlight.

"Yes!" Zach exclaimed. "I knew it! Look at it go!"

The vacuum was a deluxe model built by one of Zach's uncles, who was something of a mad-scientist magician. It was way more powerful than the average vacuum. It had been built to clean up even the most dangerous of magical messes. But it had never operated by itself before.

I'm doing this, Zach thought. *By magic!*

"Are you seeing this?" he asked his dad.

"Uh-huh," Mr. King said.

Waving the flashlight like a wand, Zach tried to control the self-propelled vacuum cleaner, but he hadn't yet gotten control of his new powers, he guessed. The machine came charging at him, sucking up dirt and dust and potato-chip crumbs from the carpet as though it was starving.

"Halt! Stop! Whoa!"

"I can't stop it," he heard his sister yell.

"What the . . . ," Zach yelped as he backpedaled and then tripped over his own two feet. The vacuum rammed into him, catching the hem of his pants legs and sucking them right off him. Zach was suddenly on the ground, on his back, in his underwear.

The vacuum cleaner choked and sputtered as the pants got stuck in its suction. It juttered and then shut down with an exhausted sigh and a cloudy dust burp.

"Sophie," Mr. King said firmly. "That's enough."

"What?" Zach said as his little sister appeared out of nowhere, standing behind the vacuum. Sophie was only nine and barely half Zach's height, but she'd already found her magic. A pair of hot-pink eyeglasses allowed her to be invisible whenever she wanted to.

"Sorry," she said. "I lost control."

Zach's heart sank as he realized that Sophie had been operating the vacuum all along.

The flashlight was just a flashlight, and Zach was still just an ordinary kid.

"You shouldn't play tricks on Zach like that," Mr. King scolded Sophie.

"I was just trying to help," she insisted. "I thought that if he had a little more confidence, it'd help him find his magic."

"Thanks," Zach said grumpily, "but I don't need your help. I'm going to find my magic soon. I can feel it."

"I know you will, big bro," she said, rubbing his

shoulder. "Don't give up."

"Thanks," Zach said again. He loved his sister. She always meant well and he knew she was always looking out for him, but sometimes Zach wondered who really was the big sibling in the family.

"Daddy," she said as her father wrenched Zach's pants free, "if you have to go help Mom get ready for the reunion, I can stay and work more with Zach."

"I'm good," Zach said, frowning. "I think I need a break from everyone's help." He tossed the useless flashlight in with the other discards.

"I'm sorry, son." Mr. King patted Zach on the back. "We'll practice again after the reunion. You just need to be patient."

Easy for you to say, Zach thought. Most Kings found their magic when they were little kids. It'd been a long time since anyone in their family had been as old as Zach and still had nothing.

He couldn't help but wonder if he'd ever find his own magic . . . or if it wasn't already too late for him.

CHAPTER 2

Even though he'd seen his mother work her magic hundreds of times before, Zach couldn't help but be wowed as he watched her magically make an elaborate ice sculpture grow from nothing but a small cup of ice water. Ice crystals seemed to dance, bending and bonding together in slow motion as her right hand gracefully conducted a silent ballet. Zach's mom lowered her magic ring and nodded in satisfaction at the winged ice dragon that now stood in the center of the picnic table.

With her hand on her hip, she asked Zach what he thought of her magical ice sculpture. Though his mother was barely five feet tall and just about blind without her glasses, Zach knew she was also the most powerful magician in the family. Nobody else came close.

"Looks great, Mom," he said. "Like always."

The annual family reunion was well underway in the Kings' spacious backyard, which was specially designed to be secluded so that everyone in the family could use their magic openly without worry of being observed by neighbors.

Everyone except Zach, of course.

All he could do was watch as relatives helped get the end-of-summer gathering ready. Aunt Maggie used her magic magnifying glass to turn a cupcake into a chocolate cake big enough to feed the entire clan. The younger kids in the family called her "Maggie the Magnificent." Zach's dad tended to the barbecue grill, using his wristwatch to make sure every hot dog and hamburger patty was cooked for *exactly* the right amount of time. Sophie was playing hide-and-seek with a bunch of the younger kids. Her ability to turn invisible gave her a totally unfair advantage, even if little Cousin Mark still managed to find her by using his dowsing rod. Uncle Herbert lit tiki torches with a tap of his belt buckle, while Auntie Annie pulled out all sorts of knickknacks and party-themed trinkets from her bottomless purse.

"Thanks for folding all the napkins," Mrs. King told Zach, ruffling his hair. "You've been a great help!"

Zach knew his mom was trying to make him feel useful. Besides being able to transform objects with her ring, Mrs. King also had her own special "mom magic" when it came to taking care of others. She had a sixth sense for always knowing just the right thing to say and when it needed to be said.

"No problem," Zach said, kicking at the ground because he didn't want his mother to see the disappointment in his eyes. "Glad to help—"

A high-pitched whistle caught everyone's attention. Zach turned to see Grandpa King running his finger along the rim of a glass cup. He was a dapper older gentleman. No matter what the occasion, he always wore a suit jacket and perfectly pressed pants. When the family didn't quiet down quickly enough, he stuck two fingers in his mouth and whistled so loudly Zach couldn't imagine that the neighbors didn't hear him.

"Abracadabra, ladies and gentlemen, sons and daughters and in-laws! Please note that I have nothing up my sleeve . . . or do I?"

Just like an old-time stage magician, he pulled out an endless red silk handkerchief, but that was just the beginning of his trick. With a flick of his wrist, he transformed the handkerchief into a pair of hanging red theater curtains like you'd see in front of a stage before a show. It was the same trick he did every year—and it never failed to amaze Zach.

"Get ready for the talent show, boys and girls!" he said. "I can't wait to see how all of you youngsters have progressed since our last reunion! Do you all remember the most important lesson?"

And all the kids snapped to attention and said together without being prompted, "Magic only gets more powerful when you do it right."

Zach winced. For him, magic was a trick that never

worked. The talent show was an annual family tradition where all the kids were supposed to show off how their magical skills had gotten better.

"It's okay if you want to skip the show part," his mom whispered to him. She knew how hard it was on Zach not being able to participate in the show. "Maybe you can help your father with the grilling instead?"

"It's okay, Mom," he told her. "I have a plan."

"A plan?" She raised an eyebrow. "I don't want a repeat of last year, Zachie."

"Last year . . ." Zach remembered the exploding-potato-salad debacle with a wince. "That was a mistake. This year, you just wait and see," Zach said, smiling that smile he knew his mother couldn't resist before rushing off to put his plan in motion.

Zach had a can't-miss idea. It would make everyone think that he was developing his magic just as quickly as all the other kids in the family. Zach commandeered a twenty-ounce bottle of root beer from a cooler and tracked down his cousin Andrew, whom he found watching "fail" videos on his phone. Andy was roughly the same age as Zach and he was always up for anything.

Yeah, the potato-salad incident from last year had gotten them both grounded for a good month, but Zach knew that wouldn't stop his cousin from offering to help. Andy loved making mischief, and he was good at it, given that his magic object—a pair of reflective silver sunglasses—was pretty much custom-made for causing chaos. Too bad that, like all magical items, they only worked for their magical owner. The glasses only made things multiply for Andy when he wanted them to.

"Hey, Andy," Zach said. "Can I ask you a favor?"

"Sure, cuz." Andy put down his phone. "What do you need?" he asked without even wanting to know first what Zach had planned.

The boys snuck off to the King family garage so nobody could see what they were up to. Zach put the plastic soda bottle down on a work counter, positioning it so that it was reflected in Andy's glasses.

"That's all it takes?" he asked Andy.

"Just watch," his cousin said.

Andy lightly tapped the bridge of the glasses with his finger and the twin reflections popped out of the lenses, magically creating full-size bottles of root beer, which

Andy caught before they hit the ground. He put the new bottles on the counter next to the first one.

"Pretty neat, huh?" Andy said. "Took me a while to get it under control. There was a time when I was making copies of everything I looked at!"

Zach was both impressed and more than a little envious of his cousin's magic abilities. He couldn't blame Andy for being proud of his talents. His skills were pretty awesome—and in the right circumstances, super useful.

"Perfect," Zach said. "Now let's do it again."

Quickly, three bottles became nine. Nine bottles became eighty-one . . . and like that, there was a lot of root beer to work with. Zach decided that they had more than enough bottles to carry out his plan.

"Okay," he said. "Now for step two."

Borrowing some duct tape from his dad's tool kit, Zach attached at least twenty bottles of root beer to his body and arms and legs, all upside-down with their tops facing toward the floor. He carefully loosened the caps on the bottles as well, but not too much. He didn't want his "magic" to go off quite yet.

As a final touch, he put on an oversize yellow raincoat

that was roomy enough to hide the massive number of root beer bottles taped to his body.

"Okay," he said. The setup weighed more than he'd expected, but then he wouldn't be wearing them for too long. "I think I'm ready to go."

Andy checked him out. "You really think this will work?"

"Only one way to find out," Zach said, leading the way to the talent show stage.

ZACH???

I can't look. . . .

Ladies and gentlemen,
kith and kin,
watch in wonder as I
defy gravity!

Any minute now . . .

Bubble!

Shake!

Shake!

Bubble!

Rumble...

WHOOSH!!!

Foaming root
beer!

Zach smacked down onto the transmogrified tablecloth, which cushioned his crash landing, as did the umpteen empty soda bottles taped to his body. The fall still knocked the wind out of him. He stared at the hundreds of feathers that fell to the ground as he took a minute to catch his breath. But as far as he could tell, no bones were broken. He rolled awkwardly off the humungous pillow pile to see just how badly he had screwed things up.

It was worse than he'd feared.

Dozens of relatives had been sprayed with suds. Dripping wet, they stared at him in shock. As they wiped the root beer out of their eyes, the curtain rigging collapsed and the whole stage burst into flames. Aunt Maggie spun around and used her magnifying glass to turn a glass of water into a waterfall. She doused the flames—and flooded the backyard.

The picnic was a shambles. The food was sopping wet and ruined. His baby cousins were all crying. The little kids thought it was awesome. Zach's twin cousins, Jeremy and Jadon, were psyched that they got to have root beer. Their mom, Zach's aunt, was super-health-food conscious and never let them drink soda. They were practically bouncing off the walls from the sudden spike in blood sugar. And both of Zach's parents had been right in front of the stage and were soaked to their skin. Zach looked at his father and smiled. He pointed to his wrist, where a watch would have been if Zach wore one, and then made a counterclockwise signal. But his dad shook his head no. There were too many people involved, and his father wasn't going to risk the unintended consequences just so that Zach could save face. Zach didn't have to be told that it was more important that he learn that magic was not made for fooling around.

The reunion was practically over before it'd begun.

And it's all my fault, Zach thought.

"So . . . no applause?" Zach asked weakly as his cousin Andy clapped for him. Unfortunately, he was the only one.

CHAPTER 3

"Mom and Dad are talking about you downstairs," Sophie told Zach.

The party had ended early, no surprise, and all the relatives had gone home disappointed and sopping wet. Zach had changed out of his sticky, soda-soaked clothes and was getting ready to go to bed when Sophie appeared out of nowhere, as usual. (There were times when Zach was tempted to put a bell on her just so that he'd always know when she was around.)

"Were you spying on them?" he asked.

"*Spying* is such an ugly word," she said. "I just thought you'd want to know."

She wasn't wrong about that. "Take the back stairs," she suggested. And so Zach tiptoed out of his room and crept silently down the stairs until he could hear his folks talking quietly in the kitchen. He could tell by their voices that they were having a "Serious Discussion."

"We have to face it," his dad said. "Zach may have been skipped."

Zach's heart missed a beat. He knew being skipped was a possibility. Magic ran in their family. It was passed on from generation to generation, along with black hair and brown eyes, but every once in while it "skipped" someone. It'd been years, generations even, since the last King was skipped, and this was the first time Zach had ever heard the awful possibility spoken aloud. Was he really the next one? Skipped? It didn't happen often, but it happened.

But to him? Zach didn't want to believe it.

"We can't know that for sure," his mom said. "He's still young enough. He could still find his magic."

"We can hope so," Mr. King agreed. "But in the

meantime, there's no point in homeschooling him. He's getting frustrated and he's making bad decisions. It's too much pressure. At this point, I hate to say it, but I think he'd be better off attending a regular school . . . like other kids his age."

Like kids who don't have magic, Zach thought. *That's what he means.*

All the kids in the King family were homeschooled. They had to be to practice and perfect their powers. Magicians who can't control their magic are a danger to themselves and to the general public. Sophie had been homeschooled her whole life—and so had Zach, until now.

"I suppose you're right," Mrs. King said reluctantly. "Being at home doesn't seem to be doing him any good, and we can always take him out of school if he does find his magic object."

"Exactly," his dad said. "But on the off chance he really has been skipped, he needs to learn how to get along without magic, like ordinary people."

Zach couldn't believe what he was hearing: His parents were giving up on him!

"It's what's best for Zach," his dad said, sighing. "If we wait too long, he'll never know how to be normal."

"I know it's been hard for him," Mom said, taking her glasses off and wiping the lenses clean. Zach knew she did this whenever she was trying not to cry. "Maybe he'll like it among nonmagical kids. He could make friends."

No! Zach thought. *I want to fit in with the rest of my family, not strangers!*

"It's settled then." Mr. King glanced at a calendar on the wall. "School starts on Monday. If we hurry, we can get Zach enrolled right away."

Zach could tell from his parents' voices that they had made up their minds. And after the disaster at the reunion he couldn't think of a good way to talk them out of it. By trying to keep up with his family, he had only proved that he wasn't like them at all. There was no way to deny it.

He was going to middle school, like an ordinary kid, whether he liked it or not!

CHAPTER 4

"Hurry up, Zach," his mom said. "You don't want to be late on your first day."

It was the first day of school at Horace Greeley Middle School, and Zach was miserable about it. Sure, a part of him was kind of curious and excited about meeting new people and making friends, but he hated—hated!—that it was because he still hadn't found his own magic yet. Going to regular school was like admitting that he could never become a great magician—and he was determined to show his parents that they were wrong about that.

"Don't worry about rushing off to school." Mr. King fiddled with his wristwatch. "Take all the time you need . . . but don't make a habit of it."

Zach's dad generally felt that reversing time too often kept people from learning from their mistakes, but today, he cut Zach some slack. Zach could sense that his parents felt bad for having to send him to school.

"You're sure you don't want us to drive you?" Dad asked.

"I'm sure," Zach said. "If I'm going to go, I might as well get used to taking the bus."

"Oh, I almost forgot," his mom said. "I got you a First Day of School Present!"

She pulled a comic book out from behind her back. It was the latest issue of *Pumpkin Zombies*, his favorite comic. Zach started to reach for it.

"Thanks, Mom!"

"Wait! I'm not done yet."

Her magic ring sparkled and the comic book expanded and folded before Zach's eyes, morphing into a one-of-a-kind *Pumpkin Zombies* backpack!

"There!" she said. "Now you're ready!"

Zach had to admit the backpack was pretty cool. He slipped it on and headed out the door.

Guess I can't put it off any longer, he thought. *Here we go.*

He was at the end of the driveway when he realized that something—or someone—had followed him to the bus stop. He stopped dead in his tracks—and somebody bumped into him from behind.

"I knew it!" Zach said. "Where do you think you're going?"

Sophie suddenly materialized behind him, adjusting her magic eyeglasses to make herself visible again.

"To school with you, of course," she said. "Figured I'd keep an eye on you. You're going to need all the help you can get."

"No way!" Zach spun her around and gently shoved her back toward the house. "If I *have* to do this, I'm

going to do it on my own. If I need help from my *little* sister, I'll let you know!"

"But—" she began.

"No buts!" Zach said firmly as the bus pulled up. "It's just lousy regular school. What could possibly go wrong?"

CHAPTER 5

The first few periods had been uneventful. It was the first day of school for everyone. But most of the kids already knew each other. They were so busy catching up on what they'd done during their summer and comparing their class schedules that no one seemed to notice Zach existed. But lunchtime in the school cafeteria was a whole new world for Zach. Up until today, lunch had usually meant a quick sandwich in the kitchen in between magic lessons. Pretty much everything Zach knew about the middle-school lunchroom scene came from watching TV.

Needless to say, he was terrified.

Wonder where the cool kids sit? Zach thought. *I wonder where I should sit?*

Kids with plastic trays stood in line for the hot meals while a row of vending machines offered a variety of drinks and snacks. Zach helped himself to a Gatorade before getting in the line. He was curious to find out if cafeteria food was as bad as he had heard. Today's menu featured something called five-bean surprise. Zach couldn't even imagine what the "surprise" could be, but part of him secretly hoped it was something really disgusting.

He wanted to hate the *whole* school experience, bad burritos and all.

A pretty blond girl, dressed in a designer T-shirt and jeans that looked like they'd been ripped by a professional, headed toward him carrying an empty tray. At first, he thought that maybe she wanted to say hi to him. Maybe she'd be the first person to be friendly. Zach was practicing what his parents had told him to say if someone noticed he was new and asked where he'd come from. But before he could even start telling the story of how his family had lived in New Zealand, she walked right into him and smooshed him with her tray. Ketchup smeared all over the front of Zach's favorite gray hoodie.

"Oops," she said with a smirk.

A gaggle of other girls, standing nearby, snickered and pointed. It took Zach a minute to grasp that they were laughing at *him*, not the blond girl, who grinned back at them.

"Way to go, Tricia," another girl said.

"What can I say?" Tricia shrugged. Zach could tell she was trying not to smile. "I didn't even notice he was there."

"Why would you do that?" Zach asked as he realized that she had just done that on purpose. She'd squirted ketchup all over her tray and walked into him intentionally.

As the girl high-fived with her friends, a sympathetic voice chimed in from right behind him.

"Sorry, dude. You just got ketchupped."

Zach turned to find a short, chubby kid about his age standing behind him in the line. He was wearing a *Pumpkin Zombies* T-shirt—very cool—and had mussed brown hair that was badly in need of a comb.

"But . . . but why?" Zach asked.

"She's Tricia Stands," the other boy said. "She does whatever she—"

But before he could finish the thought, another girl "accidentally" bumped into him, smearing mustard all over the front of his shirt.

"Sorry, Aaron," the girl said, not looking sorry at all. "But yellow is *so* your color." She turned toward Tricia and her friends. "Don't you think so, girls?"

"Absolutely," Tricia said, high-fiving the mustard girl. "Can't have ketchup without some mustard."

"Anybody got any mayonnaise?" a third girl asked.

Zach got it now. These were *mean girls*. Bullies in skirts. He'd seen them in the movies, but he'd never expected to actually meet a gang of them in real life.

Lucky me, he thought.

"What the heck?" Zach protested. "Since when is ketchupping a thing?"

"It's no big deal, dude." Aaron shrugged. "I keep an extra shirt in my locker for when it happens."

"Wait! This happens *that* often?"

"I'm not exactly what you'd call 'popular,'" Aaron admitted. And Zach could tell that being picked on was something Aaron dealt with every day. Tricia and the other girls never left him alone. He wore that sort of hangdog expression that Zach took to mean "that's just how it goes." He'd accepted being bullied as a fact of life, and Zach was surprised at how angry that made him. Aaron was the first person all day who'd said a nice thing to him—and Zach resolved in that instant that he was going to stick up for his new friend, no matter what.

Tricia came up behind Aaron and snagged his compact video camera from his back pocket.

"You don't mind if I borrow this, do you?" She started filming the boys in their gloppy shirts, capturing their embarrassment in pure HD. "Say, maybe you can post this to your stupid YouTube channel Aaron. Trust me, it's *sooo* much funnier than those dumb cat videos of yours."

Zach had had enough. He took a quick swig of his Gatorade, wiped his mouth on his sleeve, tossed the bottle in the recycling bin, and stepped between Tricia and Aaron.

"Knock it off!" he said. "And give that back to him!"

He lunged toward Tricia, intending to grab back the stolen camera, but Mustard Girl stuck her leg out in front of him and tripped him. Zach tumbled face-first toward the vending machine.

Uh-oh, he thought. *This is going to hurt!*

But instead of slamming into the clear glass front of the machine, he passed through it!

One second he was outside the machine, falling toward it, and the next, he was stuck inside with all the hanging bags of snacks. It happened so fast he had no idea how he had gotten there.

Except by . . . *magic?*

He would have been thrilled except for the one little thing: most of his clothes had stayed on the other side of the glass partition. He was trapped inside the machine in nothing but his boxer shorts!

Gasps of surprise mixed with laughter as Tricia, her friends, and way too many other kids gaped at Zach, pointing and giggling.

Talk about a first impression! he thought.

Aaron rushed to his rescue, sort of. He put himself between the vending machine and the crowd and tried to block Zach from view. A few kids booed at Aaron for spoiling their fun, but Zach appreciated his help. Aaron was obviously a good guy.

"Thanks, dude!" Zach shouted through the glass screen. "I'm feeling a little overexposed here!"

"No problem!" Aaron didn't budge from his post in front of the machine. "But . . . what just happened? How'd you get in there?"

Good question, Zach thought. As embarrassing as it was to be stuck in the machine in his underwear, he was thrilled to have actually worked magic. *If only he knew how he did it!*

He took a deep breath and imagined himself passing through the glass like a ghost walking through a wall. He had to get out before the situation got any worse.

"Watch out," he warned Aaron. "I'm coming through. . . ."

SMACK!

He couldn't really move much—just his head, really. So he bumped his forehead hard as he could into the glass. But nothing happened. The glass stayed perfectly solid and his body stayed perfectly trapped. He tried again, a little more cautiously this time, but again, nothing. The glass held him in just like it would anybody else who just happened to be encased inside a vending machine.

Goosebumps sprouted on his skin and his stomach grumbled, reminding him that he hadn't actually gotten to have lunch.

Then again, he was stuck inside a snack machine.

Oh well, he thought. *At least I won't go hungry.*

Principal Riggs had worked at Horace Greeley Middle School for thirty-five years. He was only one school year away from retiring. He and Mrs. Riggs had bought a house in Boca Verde, Florida. It was a little place right on the water. The community had a clubhouse with a swimming pool, and there was a public harbor where Principal Riggs planned to dock the fishing boat he'd been saving up to buy. He'd never been much of a fisherman before, but he was determined to start once he retired. He liked the idea of a hobby that mostly involved just sitting around and doing nothing. But for now, his one and only goal was to make it to June without any trouble. After June ended, Principal Riggs swore he'd never set foot in another school again.

So the last thing he wanted on the very first day of his last school year was some sort of commotion coming from the cafeteria.

"Trouble already?" he muttered, scowling. "It's barely even lunchtime!"

Tricia Stands and her squad scurried past the principal as he stomped into the cafeteria, ready for anything from a food fight to a kid barfing up his bean burritos. Mr. Riggs figured he'd seen it all and then some, and he was ready to put a stop to whatever the trouble was immediately.

But instead he found a sixth grader stuck inside a snack machine wearing nothing but his underwear. The kid was chowing down on pretzels and cheese curls while another kid was frantically trying to cram the other boy's clothes into the machine through the slot in the bottom. One of those fancy compact video cameras was lying on the floor next to him.

The principal's jaw dropped. His blood pressure rose.

"What. In. The. World?"

CHAPTER 6

"Thank you for coming in on such short notice," Principal Riggs told Zach's parents as he opened the window a crack. "Good to get a little fresh air in. I find that a cool breeze helps keep everyone calm."

Zach had not expected to end up in the principal's office on his very first day in school, but here he was, along with Aaron and his parents. Zach had put his clothes back on. His hoodie still smelled like ketchup, and he felt vaguely ill from eating all those Cheez Doodles. He wondered if his own mom and dad were already regretting their decision to send him to school.

Things were *not* off to a good start.

"This is a serious matter," the principal said, sounding more exhausted than upset. "The janitor had to break the glass screen to get Zach out of the machine, and then there's the matter of all the snacks he ate without paying for them."

Aaron produced a tube of superglue from his pocket. "If you give us a chance, I know Zach and I can put the screen back together," he suggested.

But none of the grown-ups took his offer seriously.

"But I'm still confused," Aaron's father said. "What exactly happened here? How did Zach end up *inside* the machine?"

Zach bit his tongue. He was dying to tell his parents that he had actually worked magic, but he couldn't say so in front of the principal and Aaron's parents. That would break the first rule of their family—their magic had to remain a secret. So Zach had no choice but to sit on his hands and keep quiet and let Principal Riggs draw his own conclusions.

"Did you know that catfish are freshwater fish?" the principal said. All the parents looked at him confused, but he didn't wait for them to answer. "If you want to catch them, you have to get up early. And you can't use fake bait. Catfish can tell the difference," he added. Zach's and Aaron's parents sat silently, assuming that the principal was working up to a larger point. But then he just stopped talking. His attention drifted off as he turned his chair away and stared out the window for a solid minute without saying another word.

"So, are you saying that Zach is like a catfish?" Zach's father asked, cautiously.

"A catfish? No. Don't be ridiculous. Look, I don't know how he got inside the machine and, frankly, I don't care. In my school, we have zero tolerance for pranks or stunts or any sort of silliness. Actions have consequences, and for breaking the vending machine, Zach and Aaron will have a full Saturday of detention. They'll be doing janitorial work to pay for the repairs— to learn their lesson. Is that fully understood?"

Zach and Aaron nodded.

Detention? There goes my whole Saturday! Zach

thought. But he had still done magic, or at least he thought he had. He wasn't entirely sure. But maybe it was enough that he could convince his parents to go back to homeschooling him?

Maybe his first day of school would also be his last.

After the day I had, Zach thought, *I can live with that.*

"Not so fast," Mr. King said on the drive home. "Are you sure it was magic?"

They were alone in the car and nobody else was listening, so Zach could speak freely now. "You bet!" Zach said, mustering as much false bravado as he could. "I passed through that glass like it wasn't there . . . without even cracking it."

"How exciting!" his mom said. "So, what's your magic object?"

"Um, I don't know exactly."

To be honest, Zach still wasn't quite sure *how* he had passed through the glass. He just knew he had done it. That was what mattered!

"Well, that still sounds like grounds for celebration," his mom said. "Why don't we stop and pick up some ice cream on the way home?"

Zach was glad that his parents weren't mad at him for getting into trouble at school. Maybe they didn't really understand about "detention," either? This whole school thing was new to all of them.

"All right," Mr. King said. "I vote for mint chocolate chip."

He pulled into a convenience store and they headed for the freezer section at the back of the store. The clear glass doors tempted Zach to try his trick again. He glanced over his shoulder to make sure the bored cashier at the front of the store wasn't looking.

"Mom, Dad," he said, "watch this! Magic!"

Before they could tell him to stop, Zach did exactly what he'd done before. He lunged toward a freezer and leaped toward the glass.

WHAM!

He collided face-first with the door, and he bounced backward onto his butt and sprawled out on the floor.

"Cleanup in aisle six," the cashier said over the speaker. "We've got another dumb kid down."

Zach lay there dazed as he wondered how come he couldn't pull off the same trick again? His parents rushed to him and stood over him.

"It worked at school," he insisted. "I promise!"

"That is peculiar," Mr. King admitted as he helped his son up as another employee came by with a mop and a bucket and then seemed disappointed when there was no need to use them. "But if you didn't really find your magic or figure out what your magic object is, we can't start homeschooling you again."

Zach knew what that meant: he was going back to regular school tomorrow.

Oh boy, he thought. *I can hardly wait.*

CHAPTER 7

Zach seriously considered skipping school the next day. After the snack-machine disaster, he was *so* not looking forward to showing his face at Horace Greeley Middle School again. Tricia Stands and her mean girl clique, along with the rest of the student body, were probably already waiting to make fun of him.

Too bad I can't make myself invisible, Zach thought. *But Sophie's glasses only work for her.*

Expecting the worst as he pushed through the school's front door, he was totally caught off guard when some kid he'd never met before high-fived him and said, "Way to go, dude!"

"Seriously cool!" another kid chimed in. "I shared the clip with all my friends!"

"I couldn't stop watching!" said a girl with curly brown hair and a Justin Belieber T-shirt. "That was so funny!"

Were they mistaking him for someone else? Had he accidently slipped into a parallel world where he was cool? Zach blinked twice and rubbed his eyes. If he was going to wake up from this dream, he wanted to do it before he got to the part where it turned bad. He was still trying to figure out what was happening when Aaron ran toward him, grinning like he had just won the lottery.

"There you are!" he said. "Is this amazing or what?"

"Is what amazing?" Zach asked, thoroughly bewildered.

"Don't you know?" Aaron stared at Zach in surprise. "We've gone viral!" He thrust his phone at Zach. "Look!"

Zach gaped at the video playing on the phone, which showed him magically passing through the glass screen of the vending machine, his clothes falling in a pile outside. Goofy sound effects made him look even more ridiculous.

"It's already gotten more than fifteen thousand views," Aaron said enthusiastically, as though that was a good thing. "It's blowing up all over the internet. You're even more popular than that hang-gliding bulldog!"

"Wait!" Zach remembered Tricia recording them with Aaron's camera, which she had ditched right before the principal had shown up. "You posted that online?"

"Well, it needed a lot of editing first," Aaron said. "I added the sound effects to punch things up and had to clean up the audio and the lens flares a bit, but it turned out great."

"But, dude," Zach sputtered. He wasn't sure how to tell Aaron that his magic, if that's even what it was, had to be kept a secret without spilling the beans that he came from a magical family. "I don't want everyone asking how I did that. I don't even know."

"Don't worry, Zach. They think it was all special effects." Aaron shrugged. "That's the magic of the internet—even something totally real can seem totally fake. Especially when you use the right sound effects," Aaron added as the video repeated the scene of Zach's clothes falling to the floor accompanied by a weird squelching sound.

Zach felt sick to his stomach. He hoped Aaron was right, that everyone would think the trick was just fancy editing, but he still didn't like the fact that he'd been caught on film doing magic. If his parents found out, he was going to be in deep trouble.

"This can't be happening," he moaned.

Aaron gave him a confused look. "Dude, what's the problem? You're famous!"

"Is it too late to yank the video?" Zach asked Aaron when someone tapped him on the shoulder.

"Excuse me," a voice said from behind him.

Zach turned around—and found himself staring at the prettiest girl he had ever seen. She had long brown hair and amazing big dark eyes. A T-shirt, cool jeans, and well-worn cowboy boots made her stand out from the wannabe fashionistas like Tricia and her mean girl squad.

"Sorry to interrupt," she said, "but you're the kid in that video, right? With the snack machine?"

"Um, er, well . . ." Zach suddenly forgot what words were. His tongue felt as clumsy as a tap-dancing turkey. "I mean, that is . . ."

"Yep, that's him," Aaron said. "Zach, from the video."

"Pleased to meet you, Zach-from-the-video." She held out her hand. "My name's Rachel and I wanted to say that that trick was *amazing*—and hilarious, too. Cool video. Very cool."

"Er, thanks." Zach finally managed to speak. "Glad you liked it."

The bell rang, calling all the kids to their homerooms.

"Uh-oh. Gotta run," Rachel said. "See you around, Zach. You too, Aaron."

Zach watched her hurry off to homeroom as Aaron tugged on his arm.

"So what's the problem?" Aaron asked as if nothing had happened, as if the prettiest girl in the world hadn't just told Zach he was "very cool." "You seemed kinda freaked out before."

"No problem," Zach said, smiling, slinging his backpack over his shoulder. "No problem at all."

Maybe middle school wasn't going to be so bad after all?

CHAPTER 8

"Michael!" Aaron yelped at his cat. "Watch out for your tail!"

The fluffy gray tabby sprang from the windowsill, knocking over a nearby lamp, which tumbled toward Aaron's bedroom floor. Aaron dived for the lamp, catching it inches before it hit the floor.

"Whew! That was a close one," he told Zach as he placed the lamp back on the nightstand where it belonged. "Now you see why I always carry superglue. You never know when you're going to need it." Aaron leaned over to pet the cat, which was rubbing itself against his legs. "Michael, you crazy rascal, you. We have company, so try to behave!"

"Meow?" said the cat.

Aaron had invited Zach back to his house after school. The two boys were quickly becoming inseparable, and Zach couldn't deny that it was good to finally have a real friend, someone to talk to who wasn't his sister or his parents.

"That's the same cat from your videos, right?" Zach glanced around Aaron's room. Movie posters decorated the walls. Cat toys littered the floor. "The ones you were showing me at school?"

"Yep," Aaron said. "But forget about those videos for a moment— no offense, Michael. They're not half as popular as the one of you in the vending machine."

THE ADVENTURES OF
SUPER MICHAEL

THE WORLD'S GREATEST CAT

"How many views are we up to?" Zach asked, though he was slightly afraid to hear the answer.

"Almost twenty-five thousand! We need to do more, Zach. We need to keep the momentum going. And if we're going to, I need to know, dude, how *did* you actually get into that vending machine?"

"I wish I knew!" Zach said.

"You and Tricia weren't in on it together, were you? I wouldn't put it past her. That girl is evil, pure evil. I've known her since kindergarten—and I don't think she's ever had a single nice thing to say to me. You know she single-handedly ruined my birthday last year?"

"How?" Zach asked.

"She told everyone it'd be really funny if no one came."

"Why would she do that?"

"Like I said, man, she's evil, man. Pure evil. Look up *evil* in the dictionary and you'll see a picture of her."

"Well, I swear she had nothing to do with whatever happened with the vending machine!" Zach insisted. "It just . . . happened."

"Yeah, that's what I told my mom when Michael broke a whole box of Christmas ornaments. C'mon, if we're going to be best friends, you have to tell me."

"Best friends?" Zach asked. He'd only known Aaron for, like, two days.

"Too soon?" Aaron asked.

Zach hesitated. "No, best friends . . . I like it— definitely."

"So," Aaron said. "'Fess up."

"Look, seriously, you wouldn't believe me if I told you. . . ."

"Oh, yeah," Aaron prompted, rubbing his hands together.

Zach glanced around as though he was afraid that somebody might be listening, even though he could hear Aaron's folks puttering around downstairs. Zach walked around the room, holding his arms out and waving them around, much to Michael's alarm. The skittish cat jumped into Aaron's arms and clambered up on to Aaron's shoulders, his sharp claws poking him with every step.

"Just making sure we're really alone," Zach said. There was no sign of Sophie in the room, thankfully. "Trust me on this."

"We're besties now, so, of course," Aaron said. "But you're not crazy, are you? I mean, it's cool if you are. We can still be BFFs, but better if I know sooner rather than later."

"Here's the thing. . . ." Zach closed the bedroom door and lowered his voice. "That wasn't a trick. That was magic. *Real* magic."

"So you are crazy."

"I'm not crazy," Zach told Aaron.

"Real magic," Aaron echoed. "Like abracadabra stuff?"

"So you've heard of it?" Zach said, suddenly hopeful, surprised that Aaron knew the secret word.

"Dude, stop kidding around."

"I'm not kidding. My whole family is magic."

"So what's your power?" Aaron asked.

"We don't know what my magic is yet. That's why I'm in regular school. My parents think I might have been skipped, but I think the vending machine thing was proof that I really am magical, even if I have no idea how I did it."

"Why are you telling me all this, dude?"

"You asked," Zach blurted.

"Look, if you don't want to tell me how your trick works, that's cool. But you don't need to make up some silly story about your family being wizards."

"Magicians," Zach corrected him. "We're not wizards—gross. And it's not a story. It's the truth!"

Aaron looked long and hard at Zach and he realized, despite himself, that he believed the kid. Yes, he might be crazy, but so what? It'd been a long time since Aaron had had a real best friend. *If he thinks he's a magician, what's the harm, really?*

"Okay. I guess I don't need to understand how your magic works to use it to make more videos."

"More magic videos?"

"Of course! We can't stop now. Everyone at school loved the last one. It's our best chance to get popular. You saw that. Just think how much love we'll get after everyone sees your *next* trick!"

Zach's face fell. "That might be a problem."

"How come?"

"To be honest," Zach said, "I'm not sure I have another trick."

CHAPTER 9

Saturday detention turned out to be just as much of a bummer as Zach had expected.

Instead of playing video games and shooting hoops and going to the movies, Zach and Aaron were stuck at school mopping the cafeteria and kitchen floors, which were messy enough to give him second thoughts about ever eating there again. It took hard work to wipe up all the caked-on food stains and muddy footprints. Dried, crusty ketchup and mustard stains reminded Zach of how Tricia and her fellow mean girls had picked on him and Aaron a few days ago.

"This sucks," Aaron complained. "Remind me if I'm ever making a list of the least fun things to do on a Saturday to put cleaning the school cafeteria at number one."

"What would be number two?"

"I'd say supergluing back together a hundred broken Christmas ornaments."

"Hey, look what I found." Zach pulled a crumpled scarf out from beneath a table. "Somebody must have dropped this after lunch."

"Take it to Lost and Found," the school janitor said gruffly. Mr. McGillicuddy looked up from the magazine he'd been reading while "supervising" Zach and Aaron. He pointed toward a hallway. "In the basement . . . that way."

"Okay." Zach nodded at Aaron. "Be right back."

Still new to the school, Zach got slightly lost before he located a stairwell at the end of a long, empty hallway. He headed down the stairs into the basement, which was dusty, dimly lit, and, to be honest, a little spooky. Exposed lightbulbs cast long shadows on the walls, while the boiler chugged away like a snoring dragon.

Zach found the Lost and Found at the end of a long, musty corridor. Judging from the cobwebs, most of the stuff in the closet was more Lost than Found. Zach took a moment to inspect years' worth of forgotten items, which nobody had ever bothered to claim, including a broken Rubik's Cube, an old handheld game console with corroded batteries, some water-damaged notebooks and folders, a tape cassette(!) featuring a boy band that hadn't been popular in forever, several mismatched gloves and mittens, and a particularly ugly Christmas sweater that may have been "forgotten" on purpose. Abandoned scarfs, hats, and windbreakers hung on hooks and hangers.

Most of this stuff belongs in a museum, he thought. *Or in the garbage.*

He stuffed the scarf into the closet and was starting to head back upstairs when something caught his eye: a red snapback baseball cap resting on a shelf above the coatrack. Despite the gloomy lighting, the cap looked somehow brighter than anything else in the room. It was almost like it was glowing.

But that wasn't possible.

Unless . . .

Something about the snapback called out to him. Zach couldn't explain it, but he felt compelled to take the cap down from the shelf. It bore an embossed blue insignia that didn't belong to any team Zach had ever heard of. If anything, it looked like some ancient mystic rune or sigil. Dust and cobwebs, along with a slightly funky smell, told him that the cap had been sitting in the Lost and Found for a *long* time.

Waiting for him? Could it be?

Don't get your hopes up, he warned himself. *Remember the flashlight? You've been burned before.*

Still, he shook off the dirt and with fingers crossed, placed the snapback on his head, as though crowning himself with a magic helmet. There had to be a reason that he felt like the forgotten snapback was calling out to him. Was it destiny? Was it magic? Was his whole life about to change? But when he put it on nothing happened. The old cap just sat on his head.

"Figures," he grumbled. "I should have known better."

Zach yanked the snapback off his head and tossed it back into the closet. He was aiming for the shelf, but his throw went off course, hitting an empty coat hanger instead. To his surprise, the hanger disappeared like it was swallowed up into the cap. Faster than you could snap your fingers, it'd vanished from sight!

"Whoa!"

The red cap fell on a pile of lost books. A snap-second later, the hanger did too, popping out of a second, blue snapback, which was hanging on a hook off to one side of the closet, where Zach hadn't noticed it before.

In one cap and out the other, he thought. *Is that how it works?*

Eagerly, he snatched the blue cap from the closet. Examining it, he saw that it was the exact opposite of the first cap: blue with a red insignia instead of the other way around.

A matched set of magical snapbacks?

Zach knew that Aaron and Mr. McGillicuddy were probably wondering what had happened to him by now, but Zach had to be sure it wasn't a one-time thing like with the vending machine. Holding his breath and concentrating hard, he stuck his right hand into the blue cap—and watched in amazement as it swallowed his arm all the way up to his elbow.

But that wasn't even the most mind-blowing part.

What was *really* weird was the way the end of his arm emerged from the red cap, which was still sitting a few feet away!

"Oh, wow." Zach wiggled his fingers. It felt like his arm was still in one piece, even though it was going in one snapback and out the other, despite the empty space between them. "It's like there's a two-way connection . . . for real!"

No way was he leaving the magical snapbacks behind.

It's not really stealing, he figured. The caps had obviously been gathering dust in the Lost and Found for years. *Nobody's going to miss them.*

These were his magic objects, the ones he'd spent his whole life looking for. Dusting them off one more time, he placed the red cap back on his head, careful not to reactivate the magic, and tucked the blue one in his back pocket.

Just wait, he thought, *until Aaron sees what I can do!*

CHAPTER 10

Tricia was the captain of the girls' basketball team and she made sure no one forgot it.

She took the in-bounds pass and dribbled the whole length of the floor. A defender played her tight, but the score was close and Tricia was determined to take the last shot before the half. She dribbled right, then she dribbled left. Janine, her teammate, called for her to pass, but Tricia was the captain, the leader; the last shot was rightfully hers. The clock counted down—5, 4, 3 . . . Tricia spun, jumped, and lofted a perfect fallaway shot—which the defender blocked right back in her face. "Goal tending!" Tricia shouted, but when the ref didn't blow his whistle, she turned on her teammates. "Doesn't anyone know how to set a pick?"

"Sorry," Janine said. "I was trying to get open for a pass."

"Well, don't let it happen again," Tricia said crossly.

She slammed the ball down when that new kid, Zach, accidentally wandered into the gym, looking lost. A red snapback rested on his head. He was trying way too hard to look cool, in Tricia's expert opinion.

"Oops," he said as he bumped into an assistant coach. "Must have taken a wrong turn."

Tricia scowled as he turned around and exited the gym. That stupid snack machine video had made him more popular than he deserved to be—especially if he was going to be hanging with a super-loser like Aaron. It was time to put the new kid in his place. *I decide who is popular at this school,* she thought, *and who isn't.*

"What's the new kid doing here?" she asked Janine as the rest of the team streamed into the locker room.

"Didn't you hear?" Janine said, trying too hard to get

back on Tricia's good side. "He and Aaron got Saturday detention for messing with the snack machine. They're stuck doing cleanup duty today."

Good, thought Tricia, *but not good enough.* She had a score to settle, and as she watched him scuttle out the side door, a sneaky idea popped into her brain.

"He's on cleanup duty in the cafeteria, right?" she said, smirking. And when Janine nodded and confirmed that that was what she'd heard, Tricia said, "Perfect. Time to have a little fun."

After cleaning the entire cafeteria and the whole kitchen floor, Aaron and Zach had to sweep and mop the restrooms too. The work was torture to Zach, not so much because of how hard it was—and it was hard!—but because he was dying to test out the magic snapbacks.

"Is that it?" Zach asked Mr. McGillicuddy, after they finally finished the girls' *and* boys' bathrooms. "Can we please go home now?"

"You've done good work today, boys. I've been watching. Just let me give the kitchen one last look and then you're free to go," the janitor said.

They walked back to the kitchen, which looked positively shiny to Zach. He'd heard that Mr. McGillicuddy liked to be tough on the Saturday detention kids. He said it was for their own good, but Zach thought it might just be that the old guy liked having company. Either way, he hoped their work would be enough to satisfy him and that he'd let them go home.

"Not bad," the janitor said grudgingly as he ran a finger along the edge of the countertop as if he were checking for any hints of leftover dust or grease. "You put everything back where it belongs?"

"You bet!" Zach was anxious to convince him. "We even reorganized the pantry!"

Zach tugged open the door. He and Aaron had cleaned out all the old, moldy potatoes and had dusted each of the shelves one at a time. He was so proud of their work he wasn't even really looking inside. He was more interested in Mr. McGillicuddy's reaction. He was sure he'd be bowled over—and he was! Because as the door swung open, a mountain of piled vegetables, dried mashed potatoes, salt, sugar, flour, juice bottles, and enormous open boxes of bean soup mix came tumbling out of the door onto Zach and Aaron. An open jug of maple syrup, balanced at the very top of the heap, fell right in front of Mr. McGillicuddy, spilling syrup all over the floor, down the hall, and all over his shoes. It was a giant, sticky, sloppy mess.

All their hard work was undone in an instant.

"For Pete's sake!" Mr. McGillicuddy wiped the syrup off his pant legs and shook his head at Zach and Aaron, who were themselves now covered in flour and soup mix, warm apple juice, and powdery mashed potatoes. The freshly cleaned floors were covered with squashed fruits and vegetables and sticky syrup. "I don't care how long you have to stay tonight. You're cleaning *all* this up!" And whatever thoughts Zach had about Mr. McGillicuddy really wanting company went straight out of his head. The janitor stormed away to clean himself, and Aaron turned to Zach and asked, "What happened?"

"I don't know," Zach said just as a mocking voice interrupted him from the door that led out to the gym.

"Oh my! What an awful mess."

Tricia Stands—she was what happened.

She was there with the entire girls' basketball team. They giggled to themselves as they captured the spectacle of the food-covered boys on their phones. Why had Zach even wondered who had booby-trapped the pantry when no one was looking?

He looked over at Aaron and he was afraid his best friend just might start to cry. He couldn't believe how mean these girls were—and he couldn't believe how long Aaron had had to live with it. *This ends now,* Zach thought. "Tricia," Zach said, hands balled to fists, "you are not a nice person."

"Oooooh, burn," Tricia mocked him, laughing to her friends.

"That's enough," the irritated janitor said, poking his head back into the kitchen. "You girls get back to the gym, and as for you two"—he glared at Zach and Aaron—"get back to work!"

Zach groaned.

At this rate, he was *never* going to be done with detention—and he'd never have a chance to figure out how to use his new snapbacks to get revenge.

CHAPTER 11

By the time the extra cleanup was done and the boys had traded their sticky, syrupy clothes for some *slightly* cleaner gym clothes, it was almost dark out. Aaron's parents were waiting outside the school to drive him home, so Zach didn't get a chance to show Aaron what the snapbacks could do.

"Sure you don't want a ride home?" Aaron asked

"Thanks, but I'll walk. My house is only a few blocks away." Zach was too excited about finding the snapbacks to be able to sit still in a car, unable to talk about them.

"See you tomorrow."

The car pulled away, leaving Zach behind on the sidewalk in front of the school . . . just as it started to rain.

Oops, Zach thought. *Maybe I should've have taken that ride after all.*

Despite the change in the weather, however, he couldn't resist playing with the snapbacks a little bit. He held them out in front of him, catching the rain in the red cap and watching wide-eyed as the water streamed out of the blue cap. He then reversed their positions so that the water flowed in the opposite direction.

"Yes!" he murmured. This was definitely magic—and seriously cool.

A car horn honked nearby. Startled, he slapped both caps onto his head—and got a face full of water. He sputtered and blinked.

"Zach?" Rachel opened the door of her minivan, which had pulled over to the curb next to Zach. "You need a ride?"

He hoped she hadn't seen him doing magic with the caps. It was one thing to share the secret with Aaron—

who still didn't believe him anyway—but he barely knew Rachel yet.

"Thanks!"

It was starting to rain harder and harder so Zach hopped into the back of the minivan next to Rachel. Zach liked that Rachel told her mom that he was a "friend from school."

"Pleased to meet you, Zach," Mrs. Holm said. "Now, where do you live?"

He gave his address and settled into the seat, trying not to drip too much on Rachel or the van's interior. He couldn't help but notice that Rachel was wearing a karate uniform. "You do karate?" Zach asked.

"I'm a brown belt," she said. "I just passed the test today."

"That's amazing," Zach said. "Can you, like, a break a block of wood with your head and stuff?"

"I could actually kill you with my bare hands," she said, and when she saw Zach blanch, she admitted, "I'm just kidding. But we do get to fight—and it's pretty cool. I've been doing it since I was, like, six. My mom's my instructor. She had a dojo back at our old home and she's going to start a new one here as soon as she can find a place. Until then, we have to practice at the school cafeteria. We have to push all the tables out of the way. What were you doing at school today?"

Zach started to tell the truth but then realized that it might not be the best thing to admit in front of Rachel's mom. He caught himself and fibbed, "Uh, just studying. I was homeschooled my whole life, so I feel like I've got a lot of catching up to do."

"Well, I guess that makes sense of it."

"Of what?"

"Your snapbacks," Rachel kidded him. "Most kids only wear one at once."

Zach blushed in embarrassment. "Um, oh, that." He'd actually forgotten that he had both caps on his head. Rachel had that effect on him. "Would you believe I'm practicing a trick?"

"Cool!" she said, grinning. "For the videos you and Aaron make?"

"Yeah, exactly," he said, more or less honestly, because as soon as she said it, Zach knew he'd have to use the caps to do exactly that. "So . . . I hear you're new in town. Where did you live before?"

"I grew up on a farm in Wyoming, just outside Laramie, but then my dad landed a new job here. So far, it's not too bad," she said with a shrug. "Although I kinda miss the rodeo and the 4-H Club sometimes." She looked Zach over curiously. "So why aren't you being homeschooled anymore?"

Because they had given up on me finding magic, he thought. "They just thought I was ready for a change, I guess."

It dawned on him then that his mom and dad definitely would want to yank him out of school once he told them about the snapbacks. Finding his magic objects would mean back to homeschooling. No more Horace Greeley Middle School. No more videos with Aaron. No more car rides from Rachel.

If he told them about the snapbacks. . . .

"Well, I hope you're enjoying the change," Rachel said. "And keep up the videos. I, for one, can't wait to see the next one."

"It's going to be awesome," he said. "You can count on it."

They pulled up to his driveway much too soon, in Zach's opinion. He felt like he could have spent all day talking to Rachel.

"See you Monday," she said as he opened his door.

Zach tipped his caps. He meant it to seem funny and cool, but as soon as he did it he felt like the biggest geek ever. "You bet," he said, twisting a smile and hoping Rachel hadn't noticed what a dork he was.

And as her mom pulled out of the driveway, Rachel waved and smiled this shy little smile that told Zach everything he had to know. Then he thought about his new magic snapbacks—and having to leave school because of them. Maybe he didn't *have* to tell his folks about them right away. What's so bad about keeping one more secret, right?

CHAPTER 12

Food spilled over Zach's and Aaron's heads, over and over again, on an endlessly repeating loop. They looked like idiots, standing there with their mouths hanging open, splattered with powdered potatoes and syrup and other junk.

"I can't believe they posted that already!" Aaron exclaimed. "The only good thing is no one seems to be watching. Check it, she's got like seven views and two likes!"

It was Sunday, the day after detention, and the boys

were at Aaron's house, staring, gape-mouthed, at a video clip of them being pranked yesterday at the school. The video had been posted anonymously, but Zach knew for sure who was responsible.

Tricia Stands.

"Okay, this means war," Zach said. "She's been mean to me since the day I showed up at Horace Greeley. She's been making your life miserable for way too long. It's time we showed her that you don't have to be a horrible person to be popular."

"But how?" Aaron asked. "Being mean is what's made her the most popular girl in school."

"Then we have to become *more* popular than her," Zach said.

"Yeah, if she wasn't top dog that would definitely drive her crazy," Aaron agreed.

"We'll show everyone that you don't have to be cruel to be cool."

"Did you just make that up? Because it's kind of awesome."

"It just came to me, man." Zach smiled as Aaron high-fived.

"We should get T-shirts that say it or something," Aaron said.

"Yeah, no," Zach cut in.

"Look," Aaron explained, "I've been dealing with Tricia since kindergarten. The thing you have to know about her is that she *always* has to be the star. But it's not that easy to get popular, Zach—especially to get more popular than the most popular girl in school."

"Well, we have one thing that she doesn't."

"Oh, yeah, what's that?"

"A crazy-popular YouTube channel—and the magic to make it even more popular." They took a seat in front of Aaron's computer, while Michael sunned himself on a windowsill nearby, purring loudly. The window was open, allowing a cool breeze into the room. Zach took off the red snapback and pulled the blue cap out of his pocket.

"Remember when I told you my family could do real magic, and you didn't believe me?"

"Uh-huh," Aaron said cautiously.

"Get a load of this!"

Zach handed Aaron the blue snapback, then stuck his

own hand into the red cap. The hand reached out of the blue cap and bopped Aaron on the nose.

"Holy moly!"

Aaron let go of the cap and jumped to his feet, knocking over his chair. The bump startled Michael, who jumped out the open window onto a nearby tree branch. Aaron raced to the window, but too late. Michael had already crawled higher up into the branches. "Michael! You crazy cat! Come back here now!"

But the panicked cat just kept climbing higher into the tree until he was high enough above the front yard to really hurt himself if he fell. He yowled unhappily; he didn't know how to get back down.

"It's okay, Michael! Don't freak out!" Aaron grabbed his phone. "I'm calling nine-one-one!"

"Hang on," Zach said before Aaron could finish dialing. "I have a better idea."

He had created this problem, sort of, so he figured he should fix it. Besides, what was the good of having magic if you couldn't use it to help your friend out of a tough situation?

Snapback #1

Snapback #2

Aaron came running out of his house, clutching his video camera along with the blue snapback.

"Ohmigosh!" he blurted. "Are you okay?"

"I think so."

Zach got up and tried to wipe the trash off him. At least there was no maple syrup this time, and Rachel wasn't around to see him looking (and smelling) like a walking garbage dump. *That* would have really hurt.

"Thank goodness!" Aaron said. "But that's not even the best part. I got the whole thing on video!"

Zach questioned his new friend's priorities, but mostly he just wanted to wash off. Something in the trash really stank. "Do you have a garden hose I can borrow?"

"Sure. Over there by the porch." He led Zach to a hose that was hooked up to an outside tap, while he kept going on about the video he'd recorded. "I got the whole thing: the trick with the snapbacks, rescuing Michael, the slapstick fall into the garbage!"

"Um, maybe we can edit out that last part?" Zach suggested.

"If you insist," Aaron said, shrugging. "But just wait until you see how cool our next video is going to be.

Tricia and her bully squad are going to absolutely *hate* how popular it is! This crazy plan of yours could just work."

Zach liked the sound of that. He was just happy his parents didn't watch YouTube.

What they didn't know couldn't get him in trouble.

Zach sprayed himself off with the hose, grateful that it was a reasonably warm, sunny day, then turned the hose on the red cap without thinking.

The water sprayed from blue cap in Aaron's hand, drenching him.

"Oops! Sorry, dude!"

CHAPTER 13

"Hurry, Zach!" his mother called out to him. "You're going to be late for school!"

"Not to worry!" Zach dashed out the front door, dressed and ready for school. "I discovered a great new shortcut."

He wasn't lying, really. As soon as his mom was out of view, Zach darted into the garage and dived into the red snapback—and then out of the blue cap, which he had left behind in his school locker the day before. In a blink, he was transported from home to school. The red snapback was safely hidden in the back of the garage and the blue one was at his feet at the bottom of his locker. Granted, now Zach was squeezed inside the cramped locker, but he had a plan for that, too. He knocked three times on the door.

"Zach?" Aaron answered.

"Who else?" Zach whispered. "Operation Sleep In was a success."

Aaron spun the combination and unlocked the locker and Zach tumbled out.

"Wow," he said. "Now that's a cool trick!"

"And convenient, too." Zach straightened out the blue snapback before putting it on his head. "Means an extra ten minutes every morning!"

Zach and Aaron walked down the crowded hallways like kings. Smiles and "way to gos" and high fives met them at every corner. The "cat rescue" video (minus the embarrassing footage of Zach landing in the garbage) had only been out for a few days, but it had already gone *way* viral, and everyone at Horace Greeley was talking about it.

Zach wondered what Tricia thought of that. *Who's the most popular kid now, huh?*

Zach spotted her hanging out by her locker, scowling at her phone. He couldn't resist teasing her.

"Hey, Tricia. Have you seen our new video yet?"

She rolled her eyes. "As if. I've got more important things to think about, like planning my big birthday bash. My parents are inviting all my friends to a party at the Tri-State Zoo. It'll be off the hook. But don't think for a minute that you two dorks are getting an invitation. My party is for the coolest kids only," she said before muttering to herself, "assuming anyone gets around to RSVPing to me."

"Maybe they're too busy watching our video," Zach said. "Like everybody else in school."

Tricia glared at him. If looks could kill, Zach would have been a smoking crater.

"Or maybe they're watching you and your dopey sidekick get doused in maple syrup," she said with a smirk. "That's more like *my* idea of entertainment."

Zach was working up a snappy comeback when someone snuck up behind him and grabbed his blue snapback off his head. *Janine.* Zach spun around and tried to grab it back, but she threw it to Inez, another mean girl from the basketball team. Suddenly, Zach was playing monkey-in-the-middle with three mean girls who had a lot of practice passing to each other. Aaron tried to help, but one of Tricia's friends, a kid named Lenny who was about a whole foot taller than anyone else in school, tripped Aaron from behind as he lunged to intercept Zach's cap.

"Give it back," Zach told them, growing more and more frustrated with every pass, but the girls just laughed and teased until Principal Riggs came around the corner.

"What is going on!" he yelled more than he asked.

"Nothing, sir," Tricia said, tossing Zach's hat into her locker and slamming it shut.

"Wha . . . ," Zach cried. "She stole my hat."

"She did," Aaron agreed.

But the principal was having none of it. "I'm getting real tired of having to punish you two. You can only catch and return a fish so many times. At some point, you have no choice but to haul it into the boat and throw it in the bucket. You wouldn't like that, would you? Don't make me throw you in the bucket, boys," he said, waggling a finger at them. "Don't make me throw you in the bucket."

Zach wasn't sure what that meant—but he knew enough just to say, "Yes, sir."

"Good. Now, everyone get to class. Before I give the lot of you detention."

The kids all dispersed as quickly as they'd gathered, and as they turned the corner, Aaron whispered to Zach, "You can just reach into the blue cap and grab the red one back, right?"

"I wish I could," Zach said. "The magic doesn't work that way. No, we're going to need to be a little craftier this time—and we're going to need to teach Tricia a lesson."

"But I thought you said we don't have to be 'cruel to be cool.' Man, I even had shirts made," Aaron said, pulling out matching T-shirts with the slogan written under a picture of two kittens play-fighting. "The one on the left is Michael," Aaron told Zach.

"Wow, you work fast," Zach said, shaking his head. "But no, I have something better in mind. Something that will make Tricia think twice before she messes with us again. It's on," Zach added, biting his bottom lip. "Oh yeah, it's on like Donkey Kong."

CHAPTER 14

"So when are you going to tell Mom and Dad about the snapbacks?"

Sophie's question startled Zach. He jumped up and closed the door of his room so that his parents couldn't hear.

"How do you know about that?" He eyed her suspiciously as he dusted off the red snapback, which he'd picked up from right where he'd left it in the back of the garage. "Have you been snooping on me . . . invisibly?"

"Don't need to," she said. "It's all over YouTube and

Instagram. Maybe Mom and Dad are clueless about social media, but it's not exactly a deep, dark secret to anyone who knows how to get online. I saw you use those snapbacks to rescue Michael—and so has everyone else."

"People just think it's a video trick," Zach told her. "They think we're messing around in the editing. No one thinks it's actual magic."

"You better hope so," Sophie said. "Because if Mom and Dad find out—"

"You can't tell Mom and Dad about this!" he said, lowering his voice. "They'd kill me first and then they'd yank me out of school."

"But I thought you didn't want to go to regular school," she said.

"I didn't. At first. But now I've got friends, and these girls have been picking on Aaron forever, and we have a plan to get back at them. I don't know. I guess I kind of like being in regular school."

"Aside from getting the whole cafeteria pantry dumped on you," Sophie reminded him.

"That was just a minor setback," Zach said.

"I know I probably should have been watching out for

you that day, but I honestly thought you'd at least be safe in detention."

"Wait. Are you saying you're watching over me all the time?"

"Someone has to," she said.

"I can handle Tricia and her dirty tricks—and I'm not ready to go back to homeschooling. Not yet. Maybe not ever. Heck, I wouldn't have even found the snapbacks in the first place if I was still stuck at home."

"Good point," Sophie said. "And don't worry, bro. I'll be keeping an eye on you, just in case. *Somebody* has to watch your back."

"They really don't." Zach sighed.

"It's what little sisters are for." She smiled.

"Not really."

"It's what *invisible* little sisters are for."

"Point taken. So being that you've watched them all, it seems, at least tell me what you think of my videos."

"Honestly?" she said. "I like Aaron's cat videos better."

CHAPTER 15

Watching the clock, Zach waited until the next class was almost over before asking to be excused to go to the bathroom. He squirmed restlessly at his desk to make the request more convincing.

"Please, Mr. Martinez. I *really* gotta. . . ."

The teacher sighed and nodded, and Zach dashed out of class, bathroom pass in hand. He sprinted down the hall, careful to slow to a casual walk as he rounded the corners, before skidding to a stop at the back entrance to the school kitchen. When Zach was on weekend detention, he'd noticed that the cafeteria ladies used an industrial-size vat of instant chocolate pudding to prop open the back door—presumably to get some air so they wouldn't have to smell the five-bean surprise. Checking quickly to make sure no one was looking, Zach grabbed the barrel's handle and lugged the pudding around the corner and into the boys' restroom. Careful again to make sure no one else was there, Zach locked the bathroom door and turned on the tap. *I really hope this works,* he thought, taking off his blue snapback and using it to scoop out a massive helping of the powdered pudding. He opened the taps all the way. In theory, the bell would ring any minute now. In theory, all the other kids would be streaming out into the hall. In theory, Tricia would open her locker and get the surprise of her life.

"What—" Tricia sputtered. "What just happened?"

Covered in pudding and furious, Tricia wiped the chocolaty desert from her eyes just in time to see Aaron rescue a suspicious-looking blue snapback from the flood. A snapback that definitely didn't belong to her. *Zach King's snapback.*

He'd also managed to capture the entire disaster on video.

This. Is. Unacceptable.

A minute later, Zach came strolling around the corner, looking way too pleased with himself. He smirked at Tricia as she scrambled to her feet.

"Oh my," he said, mimicking her. "What happened here? Is that . . . pudding?"

The red snapback on his head matched the one Aaron had just snatched off the ground. As if she needed any more evidence. . . . "You did this!" she shouted as Principal Riggs came around the corner. "This is one of your tricks, Zach King!"

"I have no idea what you're talking about," Zach said.

"What's going on here?" the principal asked.

"Looks to me like Tricia's lunch box burst or something?" Zach told him.

"How much pudding are you bringing for lunch, young lady?" the principal asked before turning to yell "McGillicuddy" just as the beleaguered janitor came around the corner. "Can you do something about this?"

"That's a lot of pudding," the janitor moaned. "I'll need to use the wet-dry vac."

"You two," the principal shouted, pointing at Zach and Tricia, "help him clean this mess up."

"Me?" Zach complained. "But I'm just an innocent bystander."

"And I'm a donkey's prom date," the principal shot back. "Get to work."

Tricia burned as the janitor handed her a mop and gave Zach two armfuls of paper towels. *This was no accident*, she thought. *And Zach King is no donkey's prom date. This was enemy action.* Zach and Aaron were behind this, she was sure of it. She didn't how, but there was something weird going on with Zach . . . and with those snapbacks of his.

She sloshed the mop around and glared at Zach the whole time.

She was going to find out what it was—even if it was the last thing she ever did!

CHAPTER 16

The smell of fresh popcorn teased Zach's nostrils as he and Aaron approached the snack counter at the movie theater. The boys were celebrating their success by catching an early showing of *Jedi Kittens IV* at the multiplex. Even if he'd had to stay a whole hour after school to finish cleaning up, it was worth it. Tricia wouldn't even talk to him the whole time. She just stared at him like she was trying to burn a hole right through his head.

Score!

And now Zach couldn't wait to see the movie—and

try out a new trick he had thought of.

"It's showtime," he whispered to Aaron. "You're on."

Aaron started hacking and coughing as though he was choking. He sounded like Michael trying to cough up a hairball. The teenage clerk manning the snack counter came running out to check on him, leaving the popcorn machine unattended.

Perfect, Zach thought, grinning.

Just like he had with Tricia, Zach took advantage of the distraction to fling the red snapback into the popcorn machine, where it was swiftly buried by a cascade of freshly popped kernels.

Mission accomplished, he thought.

He signaled Aaron, whose coughing fit halted as soon as he caught Zach's eye. "Never mind," he said. "I'm fine, really."

The confused concessions clerk returned to her post. She nodded at Zach, who was still standing by the counter.

"Sorry to keep you waiting," the teen said. "Can I get you anything?"

"Nope," Zach said. "I think we're good."

The boys were heading across the lobby to the

auditoriums beyond when a familiar voice called out to them.

"Hey, Zach, Aaron. Wait up!"

Zach turned around to see Rachel heading toward them, munching on a piece of red licorice. *Jedi Kittens* was starting in a minute, but he paused to talk to her anyway.

"Rachel, hey . . . I didn't expect to see you here."

"Are you kidding? I'm dying to see *Blazing Six-Guns*."

Zach wasn't big into Westerns, but suddenly that didn't matter.

"What a coincidence! That's what we're seeing, too!" He nudged Aaron with his elbow. "Right, buddy?"

Aaron shot him a look, but played along. "Oh, yeah," he sighed. "Wouldn't miss it."

Thanks, Zach thought. *I owe you—big time.*

A few minutes later, they found three seats together. Rachel sat next to Zach as they waited for the movie to start. She sniffed the air, then Zach. "Why do you smell like a popcorn machine?"

He couldn't resist showing off.

"Wanna see something totally off the hook?"

He pulled the blue snapback out of his back pocket and unfolded it. Rachel gasped as she saw that it was spilling over with fresh-popped popcorn.

"Help yourself," he said. "There's enough for everyone . . . and then some."

"Wow!" She dug into the popcorn as they passed the snapback back and forth among the three of them. They had a bottomless supply all throughout the movie. "This is incredible," she whispered in the dark. "How come it never runs out?"

Zach knew he was pushing his luck by doing magic right in front of Rachel, but he couldn't help wanting to impress her.

"Sorry," he said, "but a good magician never reveals his secrets."

"Fair enough." She eyed him curiously while helping herself to another handful of buttery, salty popcorn. "Pretty good trick, though. I can't wait to see what you come up with next."

"Me, too," he said.

He decided that his next video had to be the best one yet!

After the movie, Rachel's mom picked her up, and as soon as she was out of sight, Aaron faked another coughing fit to give Zach a chance to retrieve his red cap from the popcorn machine. The usher rushed over while Aaron was coughing, and though Aaron tried to let him know that he was fine, the usher administered a rather forceful (and truly unnecessary) Heimlich maneuver until Aaron hawked up something that actually did look a bit like one of Michael's hairballs. But whatever the pain, even if Zach's snapback now smelled like movie theater butter, they both agreed it was all worth it.

Zach tossed a last kernel of popcorn in the air and caught it in his mouth as the two friends headed out of the mall. They broke away from the rest of the crowd. When they made their way to the street, Aaron stumbled and noticed that his shoe had suddenly come untied. As he bent to fix it, Sophie materialized beside Zach. Aaron stood up and nearly knocked right into her.

"Zoinks!" Aaron yelped. "Zach, you've been transformed into a girl!"

"Relax," Zach said, putting his hand on his friend's

shoulder and turning him back around. "Meet my little sister, the invisible snoop." Zach scowled at Sophie.

"Invisible?" Aaron asked.

And Sophie cut in to cover for Zach. "Not invisible. Just very good at showing up unexpectedly." She smiled.

"Let me guess. You were tagging along the whole time?" Zach asked. He knew his sister was right not to reveal her magic abilities unnecessarily. "Were you, like, two rows behind us through the whole movie?"

"As if." She shrugged. "I went and saw *Jedi Kittens*. It was off the hook! You missed a great movie, bro."

"Oh man," Aaron moaned. "Don't spoil it for me."

"I wouldn't do that. But you do know that Dark Tabby is really Kitten Walker's father, right?"

"No . . . ," Aaron yelped, clasping his hands to his ears and running ahead.

But Zach didn't care. Nothing could spoil his night. "I just felt like seeing another movie," he told his sister.

"Uh-huh, right," Sophie said skeptically. She watched the taillights of a certain car pull out of the mall parking lot. "By the way, Rachel seems nice. I approve." And then she whispered, "But you didn't tell her our secret, did you?"

"No," Zach said too quickly, realizing how close he'd come to doing just that.

"I mean, I trust her. Him, too," she said, pointing over her shoulder at Aaron, who still had his hands over his ears so as not to overhear any other plot reveals. "But—"

"I get it," Zach cut in. He loved his little sister—but it bugged him when she acted like she was his mother, too.

"Okay," Sophie said as Aaron put his hands down. "Because I just know that being in love," she added, making a kissy face at Zach, "can make guys do dumb things."

"In love—oh, man!" Aaron said, putting his hands back where they were but now adding all sorts of weird sounds to make sure he couldn't hear any other secrets he didn't want to hear. But Sophie ignored him. She stood in front of her big brother, smiling that smile of hers—like the cat that just ate the canary. Zach rolled his eyes and didn't say a word. He didn't need to answer. That he blushed told his little sister everything she needed to know.

CHAPTER 17

"Are you sure this is a good idea?" Aaron asked nervously as he fiddled with the focus on his video camera.

Zach shrugged. "High risk, high reward. We need to go bigger and better to keep impressing our audience."

And Rachel, he thought to himself.

The boys snuck into the science classroom during lunch break. In theory, they had the lab to themselves for the next thirty minutes, but even so, they both knew they were taking a chance making a new video at school, during school hours. Zach wasn't sure what the next level punishment would be—suspension, expulsion, death by firing squad?—but he knew if they were caught, Principal Riggs would throw the book at them—probably literally.

"Okay," Aaron said, clutching his camera. "If you say so. . . ."

"Trust me," Zach replied. "This will be great."

Zach poked his head out into the hall and checked both ways to make sure the coast was clear. No one was around. He closed the door and pulled down the shade that Mr. Honeydew used when he was showing the class a movie. Which was most of the time. Zach felt confident that the only eyes that had seen the boys enter belonged to the frogs in various glass terrariums—and maybe Fluffy, the white rabbit that the class kept in a cage back by the windows.

Fluffy was a biology project.

The whole class was responsible for taking care of her and tracking her growth, health, and weight. But today the bunny was also going to be the star of a (hopefully) mind-blowing new video.

Assuming we don't get busted first, Zach thought.

"Let's be quick about this." Aaron glanced at the entrance to make sure nobody was watching them through the small glass window in the door. "You got the carrots?"

Zach pulled a Ziploc bag full of baby carrots from his pocket. Fluffy twitched her nose, already smelling the treats.

"Hang tight, Fluffster," Zac told the bunny. "All these will be yours in a minute."

Where most magicians would be happy just to pull a rabbit out of a hat, Zach figured he could take that old trick and top it in a seriously extreme way. He put the red snapback at one end of the lab counter and the blue cap at the other end before carefully taking Fluffy out of her cage.

Then he lobbed a carrot into the red cap.

"There you go!"

Fluffy hopped into the red cap and, an instant later, popped her head out the blue one. She looked confused but no worse for the trip. The carrot was waiting on the brim of the blue snapback, and Fluffy jumped out and ate it greedily. Zach lobbed another carrot into the red snapback and Fluffy bounded across the counter to get at it, vanishing and reappearing once again.

"Abracadabra!" Zach exclaimed. "Presto, change-o!"

Using the carrots as a lure, Zach got Fluffy jumping through the caps faster and faster so that it almost seemed as though there were an endless stream of bunnies zipping in and out of sight. It looked like a perpetual bunny-motion machine.

"You getting this?" Zach called out to Aaron.

"You bet your bunny butt I am!" Aaron peered one-eyed through the viewfinder of his camera, a smile on his face that said all his earlier worries were long forgotten. "This. Is. Awesome!"

It didn't take long for Fluffy to figure out how the snapbacks worked. She started using them as a shortcut to get to the carrots before they even landed. She dived back and forth between the caps as fast as Zach could keep tossing carrots at them.

"Smart bunny!" Zach said, grinning. "You're really getting the hang of this!"

Zach couldn't wait until Rachel saw this video!

Tricia couldn't believe that she'd left her bag in the science lab. It was her favorite one and it had all her class notes, her day planner, and her birthday party invite list. Her whole life was in there. She blamed the upcoming birthday bash for the lapse. Planning the most exclusive party of the year took a lot of time and concentration. She could hardly be expected to keep track of every little thing.

I really need a personal assistant, she thought, and she wished she had her planner with her to write down this new to-do item.

But when she got the science room, the door was locked. It was still lunch period. No one should have been in the lab—and yet, she heard voices coming from inside. Voices that sounded excited. They were hooting and hollering and laughing like idiots. *Idiots,* she thought to herself, *who sound suspiciously just like Zach and Aaron.*

Tricia's mood curdled like month-old milk. What were those two knuckleheads up to now?

She peered in through the window. She had to cover her mouth to keep from gasping out loud from what she saw. That mangy class rabbit, Fluffy, was jumping in and out of Zach's stupid snapbacks like . . . like they were magic. The same snapbacks, she realized, that he had used in his cat rescue video. The same snapbacks that had turned up in her locker the day it was mysteriously flooded. . . .

Her jaw dropped as she realized the truth.

Zach's stunts weren't just stupid video-editing tricks. Somehow, he was doing real magic—and the snapbacks were the key.

Smirking, she backed away from the window. Forget the book bag. She could come back and get it later. Now she had found something even better.

I know your secret, Zach King.

All she needed was to get her hands on those caps to teach Zach a lesson that'd been way too long coming. Tricia knew just what she needed to do.

CHAPTER 18

Tricia sat quietly in the library, trying her best to look like she was studying when she was actually just watching the door for Lenny to return. She had done a social studies project with Lenny last year and had gotten him to do all the work. She just did the presentation—and took all the credit. They'd even gotten an A. Lenny had proven himself to be quite useful. He didn't have a lot of friends—any at all, really—so Tricia took it upon herself to say hi to him in the hallways every now and then. It was enough to make him feel like he wasn't the biggest loser in school. And so now all she had to do to get him to do pretty much whatever she wanted was ask.

"Did you get it?" Tricia whispered, smiling tightly. "The snapback?"

"Yep. Here it is," he said, handing Tricia the red snapback, which he had "borrowed" from Zach's gym locker while Zach was doing swim practice in P.E.

Just like Tricia had asked him to.

"Thanks so much!" She grinned at Lenny. "I owe you one!"

"Anything for you, Tricia," he said. "What do you want it for, anyway? It's not really your look."

"Sorry. Need-to-know only," she said. "You remember what you're supposed to do next?"

He searched his memory. "Text you when Zach gets out of P.E.—and then again when he puts on his blue snapback?"

"The very second," she insisted.

She sent him off to stand outside the boys' locker room while she scurried out the back of the library to the science lab. She was skipping one of her own classes to pull off this stunt, but that was no big deal; she could always get her parents to write her an excuse if necessary.

The lab was empty, so she snuck in and went straight for the enormous glass terrarium near the coat closet, where Mr. Honeydew kept dozens of gross, warty frogs. They croaked at her as she opened the lid of the terrarium.

Lenny texted her, right on schedule. She took the red snapback out, and making a face, she reached for a frog. The frog writhed around in her hand. It was slimy and cold—so disgusting. Would it give her warts? It better not, or that'd be one more thing she'd have to make Zach suffer for. Her phone flashed. Zach had put the blue snapback on, and so Tricia dropped the first frog into the red one. *Played a magic trick on me, did you? Let's see how you like it. . . .*

"You have no idea what happened to the red cap?" Aaron asked Zach as they frantically searched his gym locker after swim class.

"Nope!" Zach looked around the locker room, peeking under soggy benches and towels while changing back into his school clothes. "I'm sure I left it in my locker, but now I can't find it anywhere!"

Aaron looked alarmed. "What if Principal Riggs is on to us? What if he has the other cap?"

"Don't panic," Zach said as the second bell rang. He pulled out the blue cap and was going to jump into it to teleport to the red cap when Aaron grabbed him by the wrist.

"Wait! If Principal Riggs does have the other cap, you can't just show up and steal it back. He'll know something is up. We'll be busted then for sure."

"Good point," Zach said as he and Aaron hustled out of the locker room and into the hallway as the final bell rang to signal they had sixty seconds to get to their next class. "We'll figure something out. It couldn't have gone far," Zach told Aaron as much to calm him down as himself. Zach slapped on the blue snapback, and without meaning to, he must have opened the portal because suddenly felt something cold and slimy sitting on top of his head.

He reached up and touched his cap—and the thing croaked.

"Whoa!" he yelped. "What in the—"

And before Zach could finish the thought, a frog jumped out from beneath his cap, and then quickly another frog, and another one. Dozens of frogs came bounding out of his cap, falling down his back, down his shirt, and then hopping ahead of them in the hallway. It only took a moment for the other students to notice and for the shrieks to start. Zach yanked the snapback from his head, but the frogs kept coming and coming and coming.

The science lab, he realized. But how had the red snapback gotten into the frog terrarium?

But there was no time to figure that out now. If they couldn't catch the frogs, they were sure to get busted—again. Zach and Aaron scrambled around on all fours, weaving in and out of the frantic students, catching as many as they could and stuffing them back into the blue snapback. Zach just hoped that in all the chaos no one would notice what they were doing. Their Spanish teacher, Mrs. Ortega, held up her hands and yelled, "There's nothing to see here. Go to class. There's nothing—" when a frightened frog jumped from the top of a locker and landed right in her open mouth.

"Sorry!" Zach grabbed the frog by the legs and popped it out of her mouth before tossing it back into the snapback. Mrs. Ortega ran to the water fountain to wash out the taste as quickly as she could while Zach chased down a team of frogs that were making a beeline for the girls' bathroom. "Stop!" he yelled. But too late.

Frogs are not good at following orders.

The screams that echoed out were deafening. The girls nearly trampled Zach running away.

And then to make matters worse, Rachel came down the hall and found Zach in the middle of the disaster. A frog landed on his head. One of its legs dangled in front of his face.

"Zach?" She blinked in surprise, plucking the frog off his head. "What's going on here?"

Zach felt like an idiot. "Sorry! Can't talk now! Kinda busy!" He grabbed the frog from her and hid it behind his back as Principal Riggs stormed around the corner.

"What in blazes is going on around here?" His already surly expression darkened even more as he spotted Zach and Aaron. "You two again? I should have known!"

Zach hastily hid the blue snapback behind his back

and shoved the frog that he held in his other hand back into it.

"It's not what it looks like, Mr. Riggs," he sputtered. "I can explain!"

The principal crossed his arms across his chest. "This should be good."

Zach struggled to come up with an excuse that didn't involve a missing magical snapback. "Um, the frogs staged a daring escape from the science lab?"

"And you had nothing to do with it?" Mr. Riggs asked.

Not on purpose, Zach thought. "No, sir."

"Me either," Aaron chimed in. "We were just helping out, you know? Trying to get the specimens back where they belong—for science."

Zach wasn't sure if the principal was going to believe them, but before he could say anything else, Tricia strolled down the hall, waving the red snapback.

"Oh, Zach!" she called out sweetly. "I just found this very unattractive baseball cap in the science lab, by the terrarium. It belongs to you, doesn't it?"

"I knew it!" Mr. Riggs snatched the snapback from Tricia's hand. "This is another one of your exhausting pranks, isn't it?" He tucked the cap under his arm. "Do you know what the temperature is in Florida right now? Do you? It's eighty-two degrees. Eighty-two—and sunny! Give me that," he said, snatching Aaron's camera away. "I'll not have you causing trouble at this school just so you can post those videos up on the interTube."

"You know," Tricia added helpfully, "Zach uses a blue cap in his tricks, too."

"Is that so?" Principal Riggs peered at Zach. "Hand it over, too, young man."

Zach gulped. If he lost both snapbacks, he'd lose his magic altogether. Aside from keeping their abilities a secret, a rule Zach had already broken in about a dozen different ways, keeping hold of your magical item was the second most important law in being magical. Fortunately, Rachel somehow sensed his distress. She slipped behind him and quietly took the blue cap from him before disappearing back into the mob of students watching.

"I'm sorry, Mr. Riggs." He held out his empty palms. "No blue cap here."

The principal scowled. "In any event, I'll be keeping

a close eye on *this* cap and *this* camera until I've had a chance to have a long chat with your parents about your behavior. I'm keeping them under lock and key in my office until someone explains just what in tarnation is going on in my school." He raised his voice. "The rest of you, get back to class. There's nothing more to see here."

A frog hopped past him.

"And somebody please round up the rest of these creatures and get Mrs. Ortega a breath mint!"

CHAPTER 19

"Great," Zach moaned. "I finally find my magical object and now it's locked up in the principal's office!"

"And my camera," Aaron added. "All because of stupid Tricia Stands."

The boys sat alone at their lunch table. No one wanted to eat with the "frog twins," as everyone was calling them now. Whatever popularity they'd built up had all but disappeared. Zach could hear Tricia making fun of them to the other mean girls. "They were infested," he heard her tell her table. Zach pushed his tater tots around on his plate. He knew the principal was going to call his house, and he was not looking forward to facing his parents. Not only had he pretty much exposed his magic abilities to the entire world, but he'd also lost his magic item. In one day, he'd broken the two key laws of magic—not an easy feat for anyone, much less a sixth grader.

"Can't you just jump through the blue cap to steal the red one back?" Aaron asked.

"It's tempting," Zach admitted, "but if Mr. Riggs notices, being expelled will be the least of my worries. My family works hard to keep our abilities a secret. I can't risk getting caught. We have to find another way to get the other hat back."

"Guess you're right." Aaron said as he picked up his half-eaten lunch and got up to go to class. "Could this day get any worse?" he wondered, and he turned around just as one of Tricia's minions collided with him carrying a ketchup-smeared tray.

"Sorry," she fake-apologized.

Aaron didn't even get mad. He just sighed as the mean girls all high-fived. "I've got a bunch more shirts in my locker if they get you, too," he said to Zach.

As Aaron headed off, Zach's phone pinged. He pulled it out of his pocket and couldn't believe what he saw. Tricia had just texted him. He scanned it twice to make sure he was reading it right. She was inviting him to her birthday party. As he stared at the text, unsure how to respond, Rachel came by. She had his snapback with her and she slipped it to him under the table.

"So this is weird," Zach told her. "Tricia just invited me to her big birthday party."

"I'm going," Rachel said, stealing a tater tot off Zach's tray.

"You are?" Zach asked. "I didn't think you two were friends."

"We're not, but I'm new here and I'm not about to turn down any invites. And I mean, it's a birthday party at the zoo. It'll be fun. What's the worst that can happen—you get a small piece of cake?"

"Right," Zach said, slowly. Something about this whole setup didn't seem right.

"It'd be more fun if you were there," Rachel added as she finished off the last of Zach's tater tots without him even noticing.

"Well, then, I'm in," Zach said, even if he knew it was going to end up being a bad idea.

CHAPTER 20

When Zach came home after school that Friday afternoon, his parents were waiting for him at the kitchen table.

"The principal at your school called," Mr. King said, frowning. His normally perfect hair was mussed and Zach could see from the cookie crumbs that his father had been really eating up the cookies, which he only did when he was upset. "He said you and your friend Aaron were in trouble again. Something about frogs and lizards and . . . ending up in a bucket? It didn't entirely make sense."

"What's going on, Zach?" Mrs. King asked as Zach took a seat at the table across from them. "You know the rules."

Busted, he thought. He had spent all afternoon trying to come up with a believable excuse, but he was stumped. Plus, it was one thing to simply hide things from his folks and another thing altogether to lie to their faces. Sighing, he realized that there was nothing to do but come clean.

"Well, you see, I found these old snapbacks at school . . . ," he said. He told them all about the magic baseball caps and their powers, leaving out only the part about the videos. It felt good to tell the truth. He wished he'd done it earlier; he could have avoided all this trouble.

His parents listened carefully. Dad went for a second bag of mint Milanos while Mom cleaned her glasses until they practically shined like diamonds. Zach tried to explain about Tricia and Aaron and how mean she was and how he was just trying to help, all the while wondering how much trouble he was in.

"I see," Mr. King said finally. "Clearly, regular school was a mistake—"

"It wasn't," Zach cut in, surprising himself. "I have friends now, Dad. Real friends."

"That may be, but the danger and temptations are too great now that your magic has started to come in. We need to go back to homeschooling."

"What?" Zach exclaimed. "But that's so not fair. I'll never see Aaron or Rachel again."

"You have a gift. Not many people in the world are magic, Zachary. It's a blessing—and a curse. But now that you have found your magic objects," Mrs. King told him, "everything is different. We have a secret to keep—and one that you've shown you're clearly not mature enough to be fully trusted with yet."

But Zach didn't want to hear it. He knew he'd messed up. He knew he'd broken the two biggest rules of magic. But he also knew, somehow, that holing themselves up away from the rest of the world wasn't the answer either. "See, this is why I didn't tell you about the snapbacks! I knew you'd be afraid. I knew you'd make me be homeschooled again. It's not fair. It's not fair to lock us away from everyone else just because we're magical."

"I know you're upset," Mr. King said, putting down

the cookie before taking a bite so he could speak with an empty mouth. "But it's for the best."

"Someday, you'll understand," his mother said, taking the cookie bag from his father and putting it away before he could finish the whole thing. "Right now, it's just safer for you to be at home, learning how to use your magic . . . just like you always wanted to."

"But that's not what I want anymore. Why can't I have magic and keep going to school with my friends?"

"That's not how it works, Zach. You know that." Mr. King held up his hand to cut off any further objections. "We're meeting with your principal first thing on Monday morning. As soon as we get your red hat back, you're coming back home." He reached for the cookie bag, which wasn't on the table anymore, and his expression softened as he realized that he had been cut off.

"But look at the bright side, Zach," Mrs. King said, trying to console him. "You finally found your magic objects. And that's fantastic news."

"I suppose," he muttered.

But he didn't feel so fantastic.

CHAPTER 21

The zoo was totally decked out for Tricia's birthday bash. Helium balloons waved above the welcome center, which had been partially closed off to use for the party. Zookeepers walked around with animals for the kids to hold and pet. There was a clown making balloon animals and another doing face painting. The Snack Shack was open just for them. You could just walk up and take any kind of food you wanted.

But Tricia wasn't enjoying any of it. Zach's "Rabbit Magic" video had rolled up nearly 50,000 views—in

just three days! Even though he and Aaron were more unpopular at school than ever, they were practically famous online.

And that would not do. No, that would not do at all.

Tricia pulled Lenny aside into a darkened corner just outside the Reptile House. She made him throw out the Eskimo Pie he was eating, even though he was barely even half done with it. "You know what I want for my birthday?" she told him. "For Zach King to get the message and go back where he came from . . . for good!"

"So then why'd you invite him and Aaron to your party?" Lenny asked.

"To teach them who's the boss. Why else?"

"So then why'd you invite me?" Lenny asked. His lips were smeared with chocolate and it took everything in Tricia's power for her not to grab his face and wipe it off.

"Oh, Lenny," she cooed, batting her eyes. "I invited you because we're such good friends." That seemed to do the trick. Lenny looked down and kicked at the ground to hide the huge smile that'd crept across his face. "So, now, I need your help with one little, itty-bitty thing—but it's going to have to be our secret."

✱ ✱ ✱

"Seriously?" Aaron couldn't believe what he was hearing. The boys were at the back of the crowd following the zookeeper on an insiders' tour. "Your folks are really taking you out of school? But you just got here. There's got to be something we can do?"

"I don't think so, man," Zach admitted as the boys followed the crowd toward the Reptile House. It was almost time to feed the alligators, and the zookeeper was going to show them how she did it. "My parents have made up their minds. Next week, soon as we get my red snapback, it's back to homeschooling for me."

"But what about our videos?"

"Can't anymore. Once I'm being homeschooled again, I'll basically be on lockdown."

"But we had such cool plans. I bought these huge balls of yarn, and I thought we could have Michael chase them and use the snapbacks and, you know, go crazy!"

"Dude, I wish I could, but once my parents take me out of school, they're basically taking me out of everything. . . ."

The boys passed by the polar bear enclosure, and Zach

noticed that Rachel had arrived. She was finishing off a double-scoop ice cream cone as they waved her over to come join them.

"Dudes!" she said, high-fiving them both. "Glad you both could make it."

"Are you kidding?" Zach said. "We wouldn't miss it for the world."

"I gotta give Tricia credit," Rachel said. "This party really is off the hook." She shivered as a cold wind blew past them. "A little colder than I expected, though. I probably should have worn something warmer . . . and thought twice about the ice cream!"

Rachel was wearing just a sweater and jeans. Zach peeled off his favorite gray hoodie and offered it to her.

"Here. Try this on."

"You sure?" she asked. "Won't you get cold?"

"Nah, I'm good."

"Okay." She tugged on the hoodie and pulled the cowl over her head. "Thanks, Zach! You're the best."

Zach blushed bright red. Rachel didn't seem to notice, but Aaron did. He rolled his eyes and shook his head.

"Oh boy," Aaron muttered to himself.

The zookeeper opened the door to the Reptile House and motioned for the kids to file in past her. Zach stuffed his hands in his pockets and shivered a bit. He wished he had a snapback to wear, if only to keep his head a little warm. It was chilly for Zach now that he was in just his T-shirt.

"Are you going to help feed Jawzilla?" Rachel walked backward to ask. "The zookeeper said we could help." She glanced at Zach. "Unless maybe you don't like alligators and stuff?"

Zach was determined to continue hanging out with Rachel, but he had to admit that since the frog incident at school, he'd been a little creeped out by anything scaly or slimy.

"Nothing scares me," Rachel told them both. "I'm a country girl. I'm used to being around animals. I used to compete in rodeos. Did you know I hold the statewide bull-riding record for my age group?"

"Cool," Zach said. "So then if anything goes wrong, you can protect me."

Aaron hung back. It took everything in his power not

to throw up in his mouth. "Yeah, I think I'll sit this one out. I'll wait outside," he said.

"Come on," Zach and Rachel insisted. They each grabbed him by an arm and dragged him, laughing, toward the indoor exhibition. "What's the worst that could happen?"

Lenny was lying in wait by the indoor wetland area with the salamanders and turtles, waiting for Tricia's signal. Kids were all around, jostling for a place in line to feed Jawzilla.

The zookeeper called for Tricia to come over to be the first one to feed the alligator, but she kept waving her off. First, she had to find Zach.

Where could he be? she wondered as she scanned the crowd while the zookeeper kept calling her name. She was on the verge of giving up on her plan when out of the corner of her eye, she spotted that familiar gray hoodie horsing around with two other kids. Hopping up and down, she signaled to Lenny.

There he is, she mouthed silently. *Go for it.*

Lenny nodded back and started toward his target, elbowing his way through the crowd.

"Excuse me. Pardon me," he said, pushing his way through. "Important business here."

Tricia took out her phone, anxious to capture the fun. Lenny was going to push Zach into the turtle pond and she'd capture the whole "accident" on video. But as she tried to get the action in tight focus, the person in the gray hoodie turned and Tricia saw that it was that new girl, not Zach.

She gasped as she realized that Lenny was heading for the wrong target. Tricia waved to him, desperate to catch his eye to let him know. But the big dummy didn't see her.

Tricia knew that if Lenny pushed the wrong person into the turtle pond, that's all anyone would ever remember about her party. She'd be worse than a laughingstock; she'd be forgotten. "No!" Tricia shrieked as she ran to stop Lenny before it was too late.

Jawzilla was in his own safe enclosure, next to the wetlands area but separate—to keep the salamanders and turtles safe. Jawzilla's feeding and viewing platform was safely about eight feet above his pen and surrounded by hip-high fencing to keep people from accidentally falling in. The zookeeper had a bucket of fish that she was letting the kids throw to Jawzilla for lunch. Zach, Rachel, and Aaron were getting in line to get a turn, but then Zach saw Lenny shoving through the line and Tricia running over after him. Rachel turned toward Aaron, who was offering her a piece of a soft pretzel he'd scored. It all happened so fast, it would be hard to say how it started or who was the one who tripped Tricia. But the end result was that she stumbled and went tumbling over the railing and into the gator pool below. Zach couldn't believe his eyes. A second earlier the gator had been snapping up its lunch in its enormous jaws—and then without warning, Tricia splashed down into the water like she was its dessert. Jawzilla turned to her and Zach swore he saw it lick its lips.

"Help!" Tricia cried as she tried to scramble up the steep sides of the pit. "Somebody get me out of here!"

The gator slid off its island and into the water. Everybody was watching and screaming, but no one, not even the zookeeper, seemed to know what to do.

Tricia scrambled backward, splashing in the water.

"Stay away from me, you Jurassic jerk!"

Without thinking, Zach braced himself to hop the fencing and go in after Tricia. Sure, she was his last favorite person in the whole wide world, but she didn't deserve to get eaten by an alligator on her birthday. Or on any day, for that matter. And Zach wasn't about to let it happen—not if he could do something about it. But a second before he could leap, he felt something grab his arm. He looked over and there was nothing there, but then he heard his sister's voice say, "Bad idea." She'd gone invisible and followed him to the party. "Use this instead," she suggested, and even though he couldn't see it, he felt her put a cap on his head. When she took her hand away, the blue snapback, the one his parents had impounded, materialized. Like magic. Fortunately, only Aaron saw the snapback appear out of thin air. He dropped his pretzel, he was so shocked.

"Thanks, sis," Zach said.

"Someone's gotta be looking out for you," she told him, and though Zach couldn't see her, he knew she was smiling when she said it.

"Hold still, Tricia!" he yelled, and thinking fast, he threw the blue snapback as hard as he could over to her.

"It's your only chance!"

Zach's toss surprised even him. It landed perfectly on Tricia's head. In a blink, she teleported out of danger. The snapback fluttered to the ground inches from Jawzilla's jaw.

The kids gasped, the zookeeper fainted, and Aaron finished his pretzel in a single, mouth-filling bite. It was crazy, but at least Tricia wasn't gator-food. "Now we just need to figure out how to get my snapback out of the alligator pit," Zach told Sophie. If there was ever a time her invisibility would come in handy, this was it.

But before he could figure out how to lower his sister safely down, Jawzilla swam over, sniffed the hat, and then swallowed it in a single gulp.

Whoosh—instantly the big, bad beast vanished!

"What the what!" Aaron shrieked.

"How? Why? Where's Jawzilla?" Zach stammered. It had never occurred to him that the gator would eat his cap or that eating a snapback could also teleport you. But clearly it could. Clearly it had! Now Tricia, the blue snapback, and Jawzilla had been teleported to where the other snapback was. "The principal's office," Zach said aloud.

"Oh, I think we're going to be in much worse trouble than that," Rachel told him.

"No," Zach explained, "you don't understand. I just sent Tricia *and* Jawzilla to the principal's office!"

CHAPTER 22

While no one else was watching, Sophie quietly materialized next to Zach outside the Reptile House. "Well, that didn't work out the way I thought it would," she said.

Aaron came out of the Reptile House with three pieces of birthday cake. Rachel was a step behind him.

"How can you eat at a time like this?" Zach asked.

"It's just cake." Aaron shrugged. "My mother says it's not even 'real food.'"

"We've got a total emergency," Zach said. "We don't

have a second to spare. Jawzilla is at school. Tricia is at school. They're both in the principal's office. We have to get there before Tricia gets hurt."

Zach saw Lenny heading their way. He looked confused by what he had just witnessed in the alligator pit and a little lost without Tricia around to tell him what to do. "Lenny," Zach told him, snapping his fingers in front of Lenny's face to rouse him out of his stupor. "I need your help. Call the police and tell them that there is a girl and an alligator in the principal's office of Horace Greeley Middle School." Zach grabbed the three plates of cake out of Aaron's hands and gave them to Lenny. "And do something with these. We're going to school."

"On a Saturday," Aaron complained.

"Zach's right," Rachel chimed in. "This is our mess. Tricia is in real danger. We have to fix it if we can."

The three kids turned and ran off as Lenny tried to figure out how to get his cell phone out of his pocket while holding three plates of cake.

The kids ran around the back of the Reptile House toward the zoo entrance, but they skidded to a stop as they saw three zoo guards heading their way.

"Oh no," Aaron yelped. "We're busted! I can't go to jail. My parents will kill me."

"Don't worry about them," Sophie said confidently. "I'll distract the guards. You guys go save the day!"

She ducked back into the Reptile House and vanished into the crowd . . . for real. A second later, Zach heard screaming. The guards nudged each other and changed course toward the ruckus. Zach paused for a moment, worried for his sister, but then a second later, he saw the guards run back out faster than they'd gone in. They were being chased by a snapping turtle that seemed to be floating on air.

"Watch out!" invisible Sophie shouted. "Hungry flying turtle on the loose!"

Zach gave Aaron and Rachel a push forward and told them, "Now's our chance. Let's go. Let's go!"

The kids dashed through the zoo and found two bikes parked at a rack by the front entrance. There was no faster way to get across town. Aaron jumped on the first bike. He knew all the shortcuts and all the backyards they could cut through.

Zach was about to jump on the other bike when Rachel

said, "Get real." She took the pedals and let Zach hop on behind her. "One of us was a rodeo star—and one of us wasn't."

"Well, what are you waiting for?" Aaron yelled over his shoulder. "Let's go!"

Zach grabbed on tight as Rachel pedaled off after Aaron as fast as they could down the sidewalk, away from the zoo.

"It was pretty awesome how you tried to save Tricia," Rachel yelled back over her shoulder. "It was really brave of you.'

"Thanks," Zach said as they whizzed down the road. "It was—"

"Hold on," she interrupted as they jumped the curb, popped a wheelie, and then followed Aaron through someone's backyard and down their driveway.

"How did you do that?" Zach asked.

"Me?" she said as they cut through a busy intersection. Cars blared their horns but Rachel didn't slow down. "Riding a bike is nothing. I've been riding horses since I was old enough to walk. But what I can do is nothing compared to what you can do. That's some pretty powerful magic in those snapbacks of yours." Zach stammered to explain, but Rachel cut him off. "I get it. It's a secret. But you can trust me."

"Promise?" Zach asked before screaming as Rachel skidded into a turn inches from a huge metal Dumpster.

"Cross my heart. Hope to die. Stick a needle in my eye," she said, reaching around with one hand to seal the deal with a pinkie swear. "Promise. Your secret is safe with me."

Zach wasn't sure how to respond, so he just said, "Thanks," closed his eyes, tightened his grip, and hoped that he wouldn't die before they made it across town.

Eight minutes later, the three kids cruised into the school parking lot. Rachel skidded to a stop at the front door next to Aaron.

"What took you so long?" Aaron asked, smiling.

"I had a little extra weight with me," Rachel joked as Zach screwed up the courage to open his eyes.

"The front doors are locked," Aaron said, rattling them for show. "How are we going to get in?"

"Don't look at me," Rachel said. "He's the magic dude."

Zach stared at the glass front doors and remembered the vending-machine incident. Maybe it'd work again. "Here goes nothing," he said, and he ran face-first into the glass doors. *SLAM!* The next thing he knew, his friends were helping him up off the ground. "Didn't work?" Zach asked, and Rachel and Aaron both just shook their heads.

"Got a plan B?" Aaron asked.

Zach hopped to his feet. "In fact, I do," he said. "Follow me."

Zach led the way around the side of the building until they were right outside the principal's office. They could hear growling noises and a lot of loud smashing going on inside. This was not going to be easy—but they had to rescue Tricia.

"He likes to leave his window open a crack," he told the others, remembering the last time he was in the office with his parents. "If we're lucky," he added, sneaking his fingers under the lip of the windowsill. "Gotcha. Help me pry it open and we should be able to get in! Let's just hope we don't get eaten right after."

If only there was . . .

. . . a distraction!!!

???

Pretty crazy birthday, huh?!

Some rescue. Now we're all trapped.

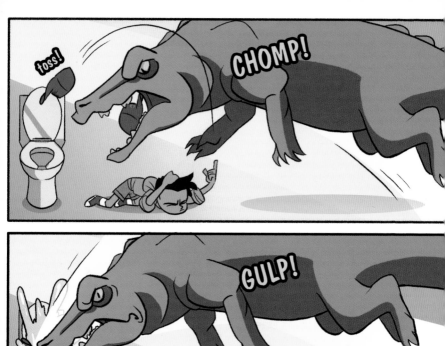

"Zach!" Rachel yelped. "Your snapbacks! What happened?"

"I'm not entirely sure," Zach said. "But I think the portals transported infinitely back and forth into each other or something. I didn't think it would explode."

But before anyone could object, the office door was thrown open and Principal Riggs appeared with the entire police department, half the fire department, two ambulance drivers, and Tricia's parents behind him. No one could believe what they were seeing. The principal's office was totally trashed—and Zach, Tricia, Rachel, and Aaron were all in the middle of the wreckage, soaked to the skin.

"What in heaven's name—? There was a commotion at the zoo, and then the alarm went off in the school . . . ," the principal cried in disbelief.

"Our little angel," Tricia's parents said, scooping up Tricia in an enormous embrace.

"Are you okay? What have those awful hooligans done to you?" her mother said, eyeing Zach, Rachel, and Aaron like it was all their fault.

Water continued to spray everywhere. Everyone was

completely drenched. The bathroom was beyond ruined. Shattered porcelain had flown everywhere. There was a hole in the floor big enough to fit, well, a giant gator. Aaron hid his camera in his back pocket as Zach pushed his wet hair out of his eyes. And Rachel stood up slowly from where moments earlier she'd almost become an alligator's appetizer.

Principal Riggs spit out a mouthful of toilet water. He was at such a loss for words that he was sputtering. "Never in all my years—!" The boys exchanged worried looks. "What happened here?!?"

"Whoof!" Rachel blurted, giving it her best shot. "I told you guys eating all that five-bean surprise was a bad idea!"

"Enough. Enough! All of you—" Principal Riggs yelled, but then he noticed all the vacation brochures on his desk. They were soaked, ruined. The principal reached for one, an all-expenses-paid cruise to Tahiti, but it disintegrated in his hand as soon as he picked it up. "My brochures. My beautiful, full-color, trifold brochures. I spent the last ten years collecting these. These were my dreams. . . . Did you know this cruise offered all the shrimp you can eat? And this one . . . on this one, they have a kids-free deck. A whole section of the ship without a single kid in sight. Can you even imagine? Can you? *Can you?*"

"Sorry, Principal Riggs," Zach began. He actually kinda felt bad for the guy.

"This was the worst birthday ever!" Tricia cried.

"Oh, honey," her father cooed. "We'll make it up to you somehow. What do you want? A pony? A new computer? A whole new wardrobe?"

"Yes—all of it," she said, and her parents led her out of the office.

"But . . . ," Zach complained.

"I don't want to hear it," the principal barked. "The three of you are on super-maximum detention until I figure out what happened here."

"Super-maximum detention?" Aaron asked nervously. He had no idea what that meant—and he wasn't sure he wanted to.

"Expect to spend the rest of the semester repairing that restroom until it looks as good as new. You understand me?"

The kids nodded.

"Good." His voice quavered as he slumped into his desk chair. "Now just go away . . . please."

Zach and his friends didn't need to be told twice. They scurried out of his office, but not before Zach snagged what was left of the red snapback. The cap was shredded as though, well . . . as though an alligator had tried to eat it before magically exploding.

"Oh, Zach!" Rachel said once they were out of earshot of the principal and outside the school. "Your snapback is ruined!"

Zach tried sticking his hand through the mangled cap.

Nothing happened.

Zach sighed. The red snapback was nothing but a wad of torn red fabric now, and the blue cap was gone forever. There would be no more magical portal travel for Zach. Frankly, there'd be no more magic at all for him.

"You're kind of a hero, though," Aaron said.

"Me?" Zach said. "No."

"That gator would have had Tricia for lunch if you hadn't sacrificed your snapback like you did," Rachel said.

"Well, I wouldn't have even had my blue snapback in the first place if it wasn't for you,' Zach corrected her. "It would have been in the principal's office with the red one after that whole disaster with the frogs."

"I guess that's why we make a great team," Aaron said, throwing his arms around both his friends. "And look on the bright side," Aaron added, holding up his camera. "I got the whole thing on video!"

CHAPTER 23

It was an unseasonably warm day at Horace Greeley Middle School. Zach, Rachel, and Aaron were hanging outside, waiting for the first bell to ring. Despite the promise of super-maximum detention and losing both his snapbacks to a man-eating alligator, Zach was happy to be back with his friends at school. After a long conversation with his parents, they decided that since the snapbacks were destroyed and Zach was again without a magical object, he might as well keep going to regular school. The three friends high-fived as Zach gave them the news. Aaron's edit of the alligator video was already a big hit online. Zach had been noticing kids checking their phones and pointing his way all morning.

It's not easy being a hero, Zach thought as the bell rang and he pushed open the one front door to the school that still had a handle on it. Zach saw the kids coming their way and he readied himself for the inevitable parade of fist bumps and congratulations. But instead nobody noticed him. Everybody flocked straight to Rachel!

"That was so cool how you wrestled that gator!"

"Did it really bite both your legs off?"

"Is it true that you trained it and brought it home with you?"

The questions came from every corner. Sixth, seventh, even eighth graders surrounded Rachel. They all wanted to hear all about her death-defying struggle with Jawzilla. "How'd you get to be so awesome?" one kid yelled after her.

Rachel put up with the attention. She even signed a few autographs.

"Figures," Aaron said, joining Zach outside the throng. "Everybody always likes the action hero, but nobody ever pays attention to the guy behind the camera."

Zach didn't mind. He was happy to let Rachel enjoy the spotlight. She deserved it.

But not everybody felt the same way.

"Can you believe this!" Tricia fumed, glaring at the scene from across the hall. She stamped her foot in outrage. "I nearly die at my own birthday party and everybody is gushing over some no-name cowgirl!"

"Just be glad nobody is asking *why* you ended up in the gator pool in the first place," Zach said, unable to resist needling her. He still wasn't entirely sure what had happened at the Reptile House that made Tricia end up in Jawzilla's enclosure, but given that Lenny was involved, Zach knew Tricia had to have been behind it all.

"Don't even talk to me, Zach King!" Tricia spit back. "You ruined my party, destroyed the principal's office, and very nearly got me in trouble."

"I also saved your life."

"As if," she said. "The whole police department and fire department were on the way. You and your little tricks, however you do them, just made everything worse. Just like you freaks always do." And with that, she spun around and stomped away.

"That Tricia," came a voice from nowhere. "Wait and see; we'll get back at her, big-time."

"Sophie?" Zach said. "Really?"

"She ruins everything."

"Too true," Rachel said, reaching out for an invisible fist bump. "She is one big old dog-pile of awful."

"Yeah, but if I'm being honest, it's my fault, too. I let our war get out of hand," Zach admitted.

"Don't be silly," Aaron told him. "Tricia is evil. She's been evil her whole life. All you did was help everyone finally realize it." Zach did notice that no one laughed with Tricia when she called them all "freaks," and no one followed her after she stomped away.

And Zach couldn't help but allow himself a smile. "I guess it all turned out okay in the end, even if I lost both my snapbacks."

"Isn't there some way you can find another magical thing? There has to be something else out there for you to use," Rachel wondered. "Like a wand or a potion or a witch's apple. . . ."

Zach sighed. "That's not how it works. One magical object per customer."

"You're sure about that?" Aaron asked. Taking out his phone, he called up the video of Zach falling into the vending machine on his first day of school. "That was *before* you found the snapbacks, remember?" Aaron pointed out. "So how do you explain that?"

"I don't know. I guess I can't." Zach shrugged as he turned to head to class.

"Remember what Grandpa always says is the most important lesson?" Sophie asked then.

"Of course—'Magic only gets more powerful when you do it right,'" Zach said.

"Well, what if he didn't mean using it right but doing it for the right reason? Like you did? Maybe that's why you went through the vending machine glass—"

"Because you were trying to help me," Aaron said.

"And you used the snapbacks to stop Jawzilla," Rachel added.

"But I couldn't go through the front doors when I was trying to save Tricia."

"True. Maybe you still need your magical item," Sophie told him.

"So you think I had a magical item at the vending machine and I just didn't know it?" Zach asked his sister.

"Maybe. After everything that's happened over the past few days, it wouldn't be the craziest thing." She shrugged. "I guess I just have a sneaky feeling that we haven't seen the last of what you can do, bro," Sophie told him.

Zach considered the possibilities. Could it be that he could have more than one magical item? And could it be that if he used that magical item for good, it would make him a more powerful magician?

"Well, I hope you're right," Aaron told Sophie. "Because it's going to be hard to top that last video without a lot of magic help."

"I don't know if Sophie's right or not. But you know what—I can't wait to find out."

"You mean, *we* can't wait to find out," Rachel corrected him.

"That's right," Zach said, smiling, as the four friends

fist-bumped together, "we."

"And we'll catch it all on video!" Aaron added.

Detention or no detention, Tricia Stands or no Tricia Stands, Zach thought as the bell rang for school to start, *this year is going to be fun!*

THE END. . . FOR NOW

KING TEAM

Zach

Beverly

I want to thank my team for all the hard work and creativity they poured into this magical book. We hope you enjoy reading it!!
–Zach King

Andrew

Lukas

Mark

Kyle

A Special thank-you to
Rachel King, David Linker, Cait Hoyt, Aaron Benitez, Tyler Oakley,
Kip Henderson, Asa Borquist, Bradley Grimm.

Zach King is a twenty-six-year-old filmmaker who creates videos with a hint of "magic." With more than 25 million followers across his various social platforms, Zach King is one of the hottest names in digital media. He's been featured on Ellen and on the red carpet at the Academy Awards—and he's partnered with Lego, Disney, and Kellogg's to create mind-blowing videos. In 2016, Zach and his wife, Rachel, competed in The Amazing Race along with other social media superstars. Born and raised in Portland, Oregon, Zach now lives with his wife in Los Angeles, California, and has founded a multimedia production company to expand and create imaginative content for fans around the world.

Author photo by Aaron Benitez

Fill your world with colour

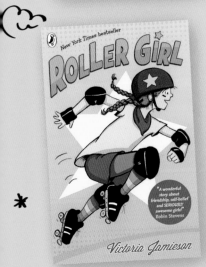

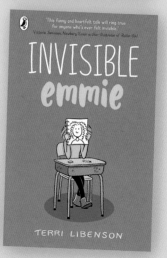

**Fun-filled adventures
with Puffin Books**

Your story starts here . . .

Do you **love books** and
discovering new stories?
Then **www.puffin.co.uk**
is the place for you . . .

- Thrilling adventures, fantastic fiction
and laugh-out-loud fun

- Brilliant videos featuring your favourite authors
and characters

- Exciting competitions, news, activities,
the Puffin blog and SO MUCH more . . .